MARO FORCED HIMSELF TO LOOK AT HIS NEW HOME . . .

They were skimming perhaps a hundred meters above a swamp. Thick-boled trees rose from dank, green water; the few patches of solid ground were covered with brush, most of it in shades of mottled green, with occasional bursts of color; flowers, birds, and other animals he didn't recognize.

All in all, Maro thought, it was not the most hospitable place he had ever seen.

He estimated their speed at around five hundred klicks, based on his own experience flying low-level atmospheric craft. At that rate, the swamp went on for a damned long way before it gave way to dry land. But when the change in terrain finally occurred, Maro's jaw dropped—the land was *desert*, with only a few scrubby bushes dotting wind-patterned sand dunes.

Pig laughed, a grunting sound. ''You like that? The whole planet is that way, pretty boy. Nobody ever escaped from the Cage, but if they did, they'd be dead fast. Everything down there would just as soon kill you as look at you. You got a one-way ticket to hell . . .''

Other books by
Steve Perry and Michael Reaves

DOME
HELLSTAR

Ace books by Steve Perry

The Matador Trilogy

THE MAN WHO NEVER MISSED
MATADORA
THE MACHIAVELLI INTERFACE

STEVE PERRY and
MICHAEL REAVES
THE
OMEGA
CAGE

ACE BOOKS, NEW YORK

This book is an Ace original
edition, and has never been
previously published.

THE OMEGA CAGE

An Ace Book / published by arrangement with
the authors

PRINTING HISTORY
Ace edition / April 1988

Cover art by Royo.

ISBN: 0-441-62382-4

Ace Books are published by
The Berkley Publishing Group,
200 Madison Avenue, New York, New York 10016.

PRINTED IN THE UNITED STATES OF AMERICA

10 9 8 7 6 5 4 3 2

ACKNOWLEDGMENTS

The authors wish to acknowledge Paul Nagle, Matthew Rushton, Frank Levy, Candace Monteiro and Sylvia Hirsch, without whom this book would certainly not have been written.

For Dianne and Love—the one is as the other;
And for JBSR and FVN—other pieces of the continuing puzzle.

SCP

For Brynne, as always; and for Dal and Stephani. Might as well keep it in the family.

JMR

* Part One *

The vilest deeds like poison weeds bloom well in prison air;
It is only what is good in man that wastes and withers there;
Pale Anguish keeps the heavy gate and the Warder is despair.

—Oscar Wilde,
"The Ballad of Reading Gaol"

Stone walls do not a prison make, nor iron bars a cage . . .

—Richard Lovelace,
Lucasta. To Althea:
From Prison

* one *

The skimmer hit a hard downdraft and fell several hundred meters almost instantly. Dain Maro felt the free-fall flutter in his belly as the little ship dropped. There was no danger; they were still far above the ground, but the suddenness of it nearly lifted him from his form-seat.

The manacles stopped him.

He was chained to the seat, wrists and ankles, and it would have taken a lot more than a little air turbulence to break him free. He looked at the gyves. They could have used ataractic drugs or pressor fields to hold him, but Omega was a frontier world, and the Confed didn't waste its technology on criminals. The manacles were molecular-stacked graphites, twice as hard as polycarb durosteel, and the process for making them was a hundred years old. Ancient, maybe, but certainly effective enough.

Maro looked up at the mirrored window next to his seat. The face that stared back at him certainly didn't look dangerous enough to be sent to Omega. The reflected image had dark hair, not quite black, and sharp features—a thin nose and lips, pale blue eyes, and a strong chin—or so he had been told, mostly by women.

"Whatcha lookin' at, pretty boy?" Pig said.

Maro didn't bother to turn; he could see the guard's image in the mirror behind him. He had mentally dubbed the two guards Snake and Pig, for their most outstanding features. Snake was a whippet-thin man of maybe forty T.S., with some kind of skin disease that made him both shiny and scaly; either that, or maybe he was from one of the worlds where the bandit bioshifters still operated. Or perhaps the condition was some kind of protective adaptation. Pig's face was dominated by his nostrils, set in a nose that looked as if it had met too many walls at too high a rate of speed.

The two grinned unpleasantly at each other. "Why don't we show him the place?" Snake said.

"Yeah. You want to see your new home, pretty boy?"

Maro continued to stare at his reflection. He said nothing. The two guards were sadists, and he'd found the safest course was to ignore them as much as possible.

Pig touched his throat mike. "Take us down for the tour, Rouge. Pretty boy, he's curious."

The skimmer began a fairly rapid descent. Maro turned away from the window and stared straight ahead. He didn't want to play whatever game these creeps were running. He suspected, however, that he didn't have much of a choice.

To Maro's left, Snake stroked a pressure-sensitive control on the latter's chair. The window's photo optometrics kicked on and the thincris plate next to Maro washed clear. Maro didn't want to look, but he knew if he were ever going to escape from the Cage, he'd need all the information he could get. He turned toward the viewport.

They were skimming perhaps a hundred meters above a swamp. Thick-boled trees rose from dank, green water; the few patches of solid ground were covered with brush, most of it in shades of mottled green, with occasional bursts of color; flowers, birds, other animals he didn't recognize.

Some sort of animal, like an elephant with a short nose and lots of teeth, roared up soundlessly at them.

All in all, Maro thought, it was not the most hospitable place he had ever seen.

He estimated their speed at around five hundred klicks, based on his own experience flying low-level atmospheric craft. At that rate, the swamp went on for a damned long way before it gave way to dry land. But when the change in terrain finally occurred, Maro's jaw dropped—the land was *desert,* with only a few scrubby bushes dotting wind-patterned sand dunes. What kind of ecology would allow desert next to swamp that way? It didn't make any sense. It shouldn't exist.

Pig laughed, a grunting sound. "You like that? The whole fucking planet is that way, pretty boy. Nobody has ever escaped from the Cage, but if they did, they'd be dead fast. Everything down there would just as soon kill you as look at you. You got a one-way ticket to hell."

Maro leaned back in his seat, still not speaking. The thincris shimmered and darkened a little, filtering out the hot sunshine but staying clear enough for him to see the surface below.

Snake said, "Pretty boy like you's gonna get eaten up by the scum in the Cage, you copy? But I might put in a good word for you with some of the guards, make it easier on you—if you want to be nice to me."

The last was said in a suggestive tone. Maro turned to stare at Pig. The guard dropped one fat hand to his crotch and massaged himself through the gray thinskin uniform. He leered at Maro, and the effect was so comical that the prisoner almost laughed. He knew he should keep his mouth shut, should just let it pass like all of Pig's other crude attempts—but he couldn't resist.

"I'd rather sleep with a genitonecrotic dog," Maro said.

The leer vanished, and Pig stood, doubling his fists.

Way to go, Dain, Maro told himself wearily. *Now you get your ass kicked for letting your mouth fly. Just like usual. . . .*

There were six of them, Stark knew. He also knew precisely where they planned to hop the wall, and he was ready for them. It had been a while since he'd tendered an object lesson, and it never hurt to remind the scum what happened to those who got itchy feet. It wasn't any particular joy to him; he had come from the military, and slaughter wasn't his style. But the rules had to be made clear. No exceptions.

He thumbed his throat mike. "You see them, doppler?"

The simadam running the scope replied, "Copy, Warden. Six for six, approaching stanchion four, two hundred and six meters out."

Stark nodded. "Good," he said. "Heat up the lasers."

There was a brief pause, then the simadam said, "Uh, wouldn't the focused sonics work just as well? And they'd be alive—"

"The lasers, I said. Full spec, full rake, full pattern."

"Jesu Cristo." The words came in a hushed murmur.

"What was that?"

"Ah, I said, copy, Warden. Full SRP."

Stark smiled slightly. "I thought that's what you said. Discom."

The warden stood behind his desk and stretched. He could watch the show on the holoproj—they would kick in the photomutable eyes as soon as the first laser opened up—but felt he should see it directly. Never hide from the consequences of your orders. He ambled toward the office exit.

Outside, the heat hit him with its usual humid intensity. He would have to get another follow-cooler as soon as he could siphon enough stads for it. The last one had given up the fight with a bang a couple of days back; the compressor had blown out and sprayed inert gases every which way. The dead cooler lay in a pile of junk in the machine yard now, another victim of the Omegan weather. The cooler was considered a luxury according to Confed rules, but as far as he was concerned, it was a necessity here. If they wouldn't give him the money for a new one, he would get it another way.

Almost time, he thought, glancing at his chronometer.

He took the elevator up to the observatory level. It, like most of the electromechanics, had been human built and installed. The Zonn had built the wall, along with the rest of the small city around which the prison had been constructed. They had been dead or gone half a million years, so the Confed extee experts said—but sometimes it felt as if the mysterious aliens might be peering at you from behind the nearest wall. Half a million years old, and those walls and other structures showed as little signs of wear as a set of new orthoskins. Stark wished he had their engineers instead of the ones the Confed fielded.

He reached the walkway. The distraction should be starting about . . . now.

As if on cue, a rumble began in the yard. A fight, most likely; he couldn't see it from here, but that's what they usually did. Not very original, but effective.

Stark stroked his com. "Be sure and get good views of the distractors," he said. That was part of it too. He hadn't asked for this stinking job and he would leave in a nanosecond were it up to him, but it wasn't. And as long as he was trapped here, he would do it by the tape.

"Of course," came the reply. That would be Lepto watching the yard. Scum who had killed half a dozen men with their bare hands would cross the yard to avoid running into Lepto when his black moods were on him. In a combat unit, Stark would have had Lepto bent to a psych hospital stat. But here, the giant Tatsuan had found his niche. He was brutal and dangerous, but Stark needed that kind of man. The prisoners of the Omega Cage were the worst criminals in the galaxy.

The ear implant clicked on with incoming. "It's a go, Warden. They're making the rush."

Stark hurried to get in position. "Nobody does anything until they clear the wall."

There was no answer to that command. Anybody who warned the escapees in any way would suffer as much as they did, and they all knew it. The rules were different here. Loyalty wasn't the key—fear was. Stark didn't much like it, but he hadn't invented the system. He just had to survive it.

The warden reached the observation tower. He keyed the holoproj on and waved it up to eight-*X* magnification and enhancement. The six escapees darted for what they thought was a hidden booster plate at the base of the wall, five men and one woman piling onto the makeshift lifter. *Probably all praying it will work,* Stark thought. They needn't have worried. Late the previous night he had inspected it personally, stuck an inducer on it and made sure the plate would do just what it was supposed to do. Somebody had done a good job; the thing operated at near capacity, the cobbled circuits controlling the repulsion nearly as well as in a commercial model. He hadn't been able to find out who from his informant, but it didn't really matter. If he was one of the escapees, he was fertilizer; if he was somebody else, Stark would get him sooner or later.

As he waited for the capacitor to build up enough charge to allow the six to hop the wall, Stark took a deep breath and felt the sweat roll down the furrow over his spine. The hot breeze wafted the stench of lube and rotting vegetation, and he was certain he would carry the memory of those smells to his cremation. They stank as bad as what he was about to order done.

He could have stopped the escape when the fight broke out; he could have disabled the plate when he had first heard about it; he could have ordered the sonics instead of the lasers. There were a lot of things he could have done, but to do so would have shown weakness, and in his position he could not allow even the faintest crack of compassion to show in his hull. If a man *knew* he was going to die by trying to escape, if he felt it deep in his soul, then maybe he would think twice or ten or a hundred times about trying.

Escape from the Omega Cage was not allowed.

The Confed officials told him that before, when he was ordered to climb into a Bender ship and space here. *Nobody gets out, you copy, Commander? Nobody ever has; nobody ever will. That is your job. We need a place to dump them, and the Cage is it. What you do to them there, we don't want to know. But they don't get out. Ever.*

The dull drone of the plate interrupted his thoughts. He had the camera locked and tracking, but he could use his own vision to see the six clutching the plastic rails as the plate lifted up its cargo, sliding along within a meter of the Zonn wall. Up quickly, cresting the thirty-meter-high alien construct in less than two seconds. Then they were over, guiding the plate by leaning, free of the Cage.

"Hit the lasers," Stark said softly.

Pig was about to backhand Maro again when he stopped. "Jesus, look at that!"

Maro heard him only dimly through the ringing in his ears. He tried to focus his eyes, and saw Pig staring out of the port. He raised his head, tasting the saltiness of blood from his split lip as he did so. On the other side of him, he was vaguely aware of Snake staring through the port also.

He saw several things at once: The prison itself, constructed of some dark, almost glistening material, unlike anything he had ever before seen. It crouched upon the ground like a predatory beast squatting on its haunches. There were other buildings and additions to the main structures, obviously man-made, but it was the wall itself that caught his attention first.

Then, suddenly, the air next to the wall was filled with lances of coherent red beams. Lasers, he realized. The pattern of the lines formed a tight net that would allow nothing larger than a bird to escape their touch.

In the middle of the brilliant display, Maro saw what had saved him from further abuse at Pig's hands; a small craft loaded with people, smoking and falling. The dance of fiery light continued as the thing fell, baking those on board, stroking their blackened forms with more heat, shining through the charred flesh with a ruby glow that was interrupted by frothy bubbles of the same color.

Maro tried to turn away, but found he was unable to do so. The execution held him with awful fascination.

The ship—it was no more than a stripped hopper plate, he realized—struck the ground just beyond the wall. The bodies tumbled off, some landing as much as fifty or sixty meters away. Parts of the roasted meat fell off when they hit.

The skimmer banked, and Maro could no longer see the results of the laser barrage. He knew, however, that no one could have survived it.

Behind him, Snake quietly said, "Stupid bastards. They never had a chance."

Pig, his face alight with a sick and twisted joy, grinned at Maro. "Welcome to the Omega Cage, pretty boy."

Maro leaned back in his chair and stared at his manacles. He had been interned before, but the reality of his situation finally sank in as he replayed what he had just seen. Escape wouldn't be easy.

It might take a while.

∗ two ∗

The processing seemed almost perfunctory when compared to some other cages into which Maro had been filed. He already had the haircut, so they didn't bother with that. A bored guard ran Maro's left wrist under a viral scanner and the digital ID coded into the prisoner's pisiform bone made the audio squeal. On his scanner, the guard would be seeing a quick biograph appear: retinal prints, EEG patterns, history, and so forth.

"Maro, Dain," the guard said. "MMF, and life."

MMF: murder most foul. It had a quaint sound to it, Maro thought, a pre-space feeling that went along with colorful costumes and riding on beasts or under steam or fossil power. The sentence was worth a trip to the Omega Cage, though. Ordinary murder—whatever that was—wouldn't do it. Maro had killed people in his time, though never for money and not without his own life on the line. This particular crime was a set-up; of it, at least, he was as innocent as an uncoded viral computer. He had enemies, though . . .

The guard interrupted his thoughts. "Pass him through. Standard chem wash and irradiate."

Pig grinned. "Strip, pretty boy."

Wordlessly, Maro did as ordered. He was in pretty good shape, despite the three months of lock-time before the trial. He had had enough room to do basic flex and kata in his cell, and he'd been in good condition when they had caught him. *If you'd been in top condition,* he thought ironically, *maybe they wouldn't have caught you . . .*

"Inside."

The small room was windowless and dark, and the jets started spraying as soon as he was inside, even before the warped plastic door slid completely shut. Detox red first, with that alcohol-pine smell and the uncomfortable tingle on his bare skin. The crimson mist stopped, and was followed immediately by a yellow spray, probably some fungicide. He closed his eyes, but not quickly enough to keep them from stinging. The air now smelled like burning insulation.

Finally the chem wash stopped and a glare filled the room. Maro kept his eyes shut tight as the irradiant bathed him. Most of his internal flora would die from the radiation; he'd have diarrhea for a few days until he could grow more *E. coli*.

"Out," Pig commanded over a scratchy speaker.

The guard held a set of cheap, blue prison orthoskins and slippers crumpled in one hand. He tossed them at Maro. Pig said, "That's it, pretty boy, you're in." He turned and started to saunter away as Maro began to dress, adding casually over his shoulder, "You got gods, you'd better pray to 'em."

Warden Stark was on his feet, staring through the window behind his desk, when Maro arrived. Neither man spoke for several moments, nor did Stark turn to face the new prisoner. Either he was brave, stupid, or there was some kind of protective gear set up in the office, Maro figured.

"Zap fields," the warden said, still looking at the yard

through his window, as though he had read Maro's mind. He turned to face the prisoner. "And the view is protected by five centimeter-thick densecris." He rapped the middle knuckle of his right forefinger against the clear material. It gave off a metallic tone, almost like a gong. "Somebody lined up on me with a jury-rigged rocket launcher, once. Didn't even crack the crystal."

Maro said nothing, only waited.

"The point is," Stark continued, "that I'm running things here until the Confed, in its wisdom, decides to send me elsewhere. And while I'm here, *everybody* answers to me. I'm a fair man. You stay out of trouble, mind your exhaust, and you stay healthy. You give me trouble, and I can turn you into puree, you copy?"

Maro nodded. "I hear you."

Stark nodded. "Good. I read your stats. You should have stayed in smuggling. We've got a city full of killers here, and some of them could swat you dead backhanded without raising a sweat. You're here forever, Maro; get used to it. I see you've escaped from a couple of the backwater lockups where you were caught. That won't happen here."

Maro said nothing. He'd heard this speech before.

"You have something the Confed wants," Stark continued. "Information on Black Sun. They are sending a man to . . . discuss it with you. That doesn't matter. You are mine until he gets here, and if you survive his questioning, you are mine when he leaves. Make it easy on yourself or make it hard, I don't care—it's up to you. That's all."

Stark turned back to the window, and Maro started to leave. The door slid open, and—"

The most beautiful woman he had ever seen stepped inside.

She was an albino. Her hair, worn down to the middle of her back, was as white as frozen CO_2; her skin was smooth and flawless, and her eyes were an impossible blue, as icy as a glacier. She was maybe a hundred and sixty centimeters tall, and might go fifty-five kilos. She wore a prison orthoskin, as he did, but it had been tailored to her form, revealing a flare of hip and shoulder and breast that almost literally took his breath away. Of a moment, Maro found his heart pounding and his mind clutched by a surge of lust unlike anything he had ever before felt.

He had been with dozens of women, some of whom had been professionals at every aspect of sexuality to orgasm and beyond, but none of them had ever had the hard visceral effect this woman had on him now. He wanted to grab her, pull her to him and take her, then and there, and to Deep with the consequences.

Dimly, as from a great distance, he heard Stark say behind him, "Ah, Juete."

Shoo-et-tay. What—?

A guard appeared in the doorway behind the incredible woman. "Let's go," he said. It took a second for Maro to realize the guard was speaking to him. As he left, he turned to stare at the woman before the door slid closed to hide her from him. He felt shaken, as though he'd been punched in the solar plexus and still couldn't quite catch his wind.

The guard looked at him and laughed, a nasty sound. He knew something Maro didn't about this, and, more than anything, the smuggler wanted to find out what it was. But he said nothing. He would be damned if he would ask and thus put himself in debt. He didn't want to owe anybody anything.

Not yet, anyway . . .

Stark moved to the albino woman, put his arms around her and kissed her passionately, thrusting his tongue deep into her mouth. She responded mechanically, like a robot whose timing was a second slow. He felt the usual stab of disappointment, but he continued the kiss for a moment before breaking off and smiling, not letting her see how it bothered him. Some day, he told himself; some day she would come to him willingly. He loved her, and therefore, given enough time, she would learn to love him.

"Who was that?" she asked. Casually, as if she cared not at all to know.

"Nobody," Stark replied, feeling a pang of jealousy. She was an Exotic, he knew, and it was bred into her genes what she did, but he still hated the idea of her with any other man. *Hated* it. But at the same time he felt his passion rising at the thought. He grew hard, visualizing Juete with Maro.

He took her hand and guided it to his crotch. She began to stroke him. After a moment, he saw the flush that showed she was excited too. Stark smiled. She might not love him, but he triggered her responses quickly enough.

"Take off your clothes," he said. "I want to see you."

Quickly, she complied. So pale, so beautiful, the thatch of downy white at her mons barely covering her labia—gods, he couldn't wait! Stark pulled her to him and lifted her from the floor, holding tightly to her buttocks as he pressed himself, still dressed, against her. Juete gasped at the fierceness of it, and he smiled into her white hair as he bit her neck.

The cell they gave him was not as bad as some he had been in. It was three meters by three meters square, close to the same height. The front wall was finger-thick durasteel diamond-patterned mesh; the two side walls and ceiling were ferrofoam slabs with stacked-carbon stringer cord bracing; the back wall was of that strange material that made up large sections of the prison. Curious, he moved closer and examined it. It was oddly featureless and nonreflective, looking as much like the still surface of a midnight lake as metal. He touched it, then snatched his hand away. It was surprisingly cold.

In one corner was a tiled squat, probably white once but now a dull gray. A single hole in the center of the slightly concave utility served as both excreta portal and drain; there was a showerhead mounted on the wall with a single button control.

On the opposite side of the cell was a cot, chain-folded against the wall to allow more space. No sink, no mirror, but an open-faced cabinet held a towel, a tube of soap, another of depil, and a roll of tissue.

Maro walked to the cabinet and pulled off several sheets of tissue. He then moved to the squat and dropped the pulpy paper into the hole. There came a slight grinding noise as the disposal unit kicked on. Standard prison issue. Anything small enough to be shoved down that hole wasn't going to stop it up, not with an industrial-grade grinder working in it. Welcome home, Dain. Well, at least he wasn't going to have a roommate to deal with.

Abruptly, from across the corridor, Maro heard somebody yell, "New meat! Hey, copy all, new meat in the Redhead's dump!"

He looked up to see a fat, droll-looking man of about fifty T.S. standing at the mesh of the cell across the corridor, staring at him.

"The tag's Berque," the fat man said. "You got an unlucky dump, f'lo'man. The Redhead, he got cooked going over the wall this morning."

"I saw it," Maro said.

"Yeah?" The man who called himself Berque ran chubby fingers through his greasy brown hair. "So we all did, f'lo'man. The warden, he had it cast on full holoproj ten minutes after it went up."

"I saw it coming in. Live."

"Juicy, hey?"

Maro turned away. The look on Berque's face made him

want to gag. He'd met too many people—women as well as men—who enjoyed watching pain and death. He remembered what Stark had said: this place was full of killers. Some of them might have been dropped-shot as he had been, but most of them had, no doubt, enjoyed their crimes. A careless move could get him killed. Not a pleasant thought, to die in the Omega Cage. Death came to everyone, and Maro never considered himself a coward, but it would be stupid to meet his end in this forsaken hole—and worse to do it as the result of being framed for something he hadn't done.

Across the way, Berque said, "Hey, hey, don't take me wrong! It was a terrible thing, terrible!" His tone of voice sounded sympathetic, but the shift was altogether too artful for Maro to believe in. Berque was a man to trust for less distance then he could be thrown one-handed, and one not to turn an unprotected back to under any circumstances, Maro figured.

He unfolded the cot from the wall and snapped it into position. His new bed was of slunglas struts and rip-stop synthetic cloth, he saw, and not likely to come apart without sharp tools and muscle. If he had the tools, he likely wouldn't need the cot's materials; still, it was something to keep in mind.

Maro stretched out on the cot. Not too bad. He was tired; might as well rest while he could. He triggered a mental relaxation drill and, in a few minutes, was deep in sleep. He dreamed of the albino woman—and other things.

* three *

A hand wand, a goddamned short-range hand wand, was all he had had when it went sour. Maro hadn't wanted to spook the buyer, so he'd left his heavy *skjuta* neatly tucked away on his ship. The stubby automatic pistol shotgun held six rounds in its magazine, each shell loaded with five 9mm steel balls. He could have cleared the room with it and been gone. *If* he had had it—

Might as well wish for a tactical nuke, he thought as he scrambled for the fresher. There were enough people in the dimly lit port bar to impede the cools' progress as they chased the four men and two women who'd been at Maro's table. The hand wand was low-powered and small, a sleeve gun whose pulse would knock a man senseless across a table, but outside of three meters, he might as well throw the fucking thing. As he cleared the fresher's door, he pulled the weapon and thumbed the safety off.

The window was cheap plastic, impervious to the occasional drunk who might pitch a glass at it, but not designed to withstand a major assault. Maro tore the fire extinguisher from the wall over the stagnant urinal and threw it. The clear plastic window popped out in a single piece and clattered outside on the alley's surface, followed by the heavy cannister. Maro didn't hesitate, but ran and jumped for the window. There would be cools at the entrance and exit, but maybe they wouldn't think to cover the fresher. It was his only chance.

The opening was tight; he scraped one shoulder squeezing through. As he dragged his hips over the sill he heard somebody yelling behind him.

"Police! Hold it!"

He didn't try to turn, but continued through head first. Fortunately, the window was high enough so that his feet cleared the opening in time for him to tuck and roll as he hit the alley's floor. He would have sprinted away, but he knew the cool would get a shot through the fresher's window before he could get past the mouth of the alley. So instead of running, Maro finished the roll, banging his hip on the fire extinguisher, and shoved himself back against the wall in a crouch. He slammed into the fake brick under the window and dropped to a sitting position, then looked up.

The cool was beefy, but fast. He jammed his right arm and shoulder through the opening, followed by his head. Too big to get through, Maro figured, but small enough to use the handgun he clutched. A 6mm needler, probably loading shocktox.

Before he could look around, Maro raised his hand wand and thumbed the firing stud. The flash hit the cool and he screamed and fell back into the fresher, dropping the needler. He'd be numb everywhere the hand wand's electronic bath touched him, but he hadn't taken a full body jolt. If he had a backup piece, his left arm was still good—

Maro snatched up the fallen needler and ran. The reflected light from the huge ringed gas giant that dominated the night sky made it impossible to hide in the shadows. Nobody was watching the alley, but when he cleared the end at a dead run, a cool leaning against a flitter spotted him. He went for his sidearm, but Maro raised the needler and fired it on full auto, waving it back and forth. At least one of the hail of flechettes got past the armor, for the cool doubled up in sudden paralysis and rolled onto the hood of the flitter.

The needler in his hand started to beep. *Ah, shit!* He hadn't thought the police on this one-rocket planet would have personally coded hand weapons. He flung it away into the darkness; in another ten seconds it would be a puddle of molten plastic and metal. He was lucky he'd managed to fire it at all before the self-destruct circuit was triggered.

His ship, he had to get to his ship! The planet didn't space much of a navy; if he could lift and clear air defenses, he could outrun their lumbering cruisers. This port city of Kito Mfalme—King's Jewel, the natives called it—had the only spaceport in the western hemisphere. Once he got to his ship, his chances would be vastly improved.

As Maro ran through the dim streets, he wondered which of the others had turned them in. It *had* to be a set-up. Benares wouldn't have done it; he was going to make a nice profit and money was his god; Lunt wanted those contraindicated virals so bad he would have thrown his balls in as part of the deal, so he couldn't see Lunt opting for cool interference; that left Morrel and the two women, none of whom Maro knew. It must have been one of them. All had been vouched for, of course, but that meant little. Obviously.

He had deliberately hangared his ship in the run-down section of the port, the part that had once been a military section and was now gone mostly to rust and warp. Aside from being poorly lit and watched, the hangar backed up to the perimeter fence. Before leaving the area, Maro had rigged a roll-up cable and extender from the hangar roof, set to a sonic switch. A good smuggler tried to cover as many of his bets as possible. He grinned as he thought of it. Always leave the back door open, old Vickers had taught him, and that's what he'd done.

The place he had chosen lay in the dark between two pools of HT light. Maro looked around, saw that he wasn't being followed, and took a few seconds to catch his breath. The three-meter-tall mesh fence, despite its age and apparent lack of maintenance, carried a heart-stopping electrical charge. Such current discouraged climbers, but he had allowed for that.

Maro took a deep breath and whistled: three short notes, then one final long note. From the roof five meters above him, the extender clicked on and a plastic rod telescoped outward. After a moment a thick coil of synsilk rope began to extrude from the end of the extender like paste from a tube. It only took a few seconds for the rope to reach him. Maro began to climb, hand over hand. He was a good meter away from the fence, but he moved carefully despite that.

Once on the roof, it was easy enough to retract the extender and climb down the rope on the inside of the fence. On the ground, he moved cautiously around the hangar. It was quiet inside, and only walkway lighting cast its faint glow along the floor. There stood his ship, the *Volny Vickers,* a converted minesweeper that looked as if it was due to be cut up for scrap. Right now, however, he could not imagine anything looking better to him.

He wasn't scheduled to leave for a week, so there was no dins working on his ship. He had enough fuel to reach either Mtu or the Green Moon, and no one on either of those worlds was looking for him. From there he could bend space and head for either the Nazo System or the Svare Star Group, leaving the Bibi Arusi System behind like a bad memory.

Maro cycled the lock open, ordered the computer to begin powering up, and headed for the control room. Once in his form chair, he felt a thousand percent better. "Calculate a polar slingshot orbit," he told the computer.

From behind him, a voice said, "Going somewhere, cool killer?"

Maro was very careful not to move.

"I ought to burn you where you sit," the voice continued. "They don't like murderers in the King's Jewel. Especially when you kill one of their own."

"Can I turn around?"

"Yeah—slowly and with great care."

Maro turned the form chair and found himself facing a tall and aristocratic-looking man, wearing a skinmask and holding a heavy-bore pellet pistol pointed at him.

"That officer you shot in the fresher died, you know."

Maro shook his head. "No way. Nobody dies from a hand wand pulse, especially a partial flash on low power."

"Sue the manufacturer. He's dead and you did it, as far as the local police are concerned."

Maro stared at the man. Why would a cool care if somebody saw his face? "You're not police. Who are you?"

The face under the mask grinned. "Clever boy, aren't you? But not so clever as to avoid treading in places you'd been warned to avoid, eh?"

Maro took a deep breath. "Black Sun," he said.

"We don't like that name much. We prefer to be called the 'Corporation.' "

"You set me up."

"Let's just say that you freelance smugglers are going to have to learn company policy—and you're this week's example. You are going to go away, Maro. As far away as one can get."

Maro gathered himself. Maybe he could distract the man. He was only about three meters away—

"Don't bother," the masked man said. "I'd just as soon shoot you, though my orders didn't specify that option if it could be avoided. No, we need our show trial and conviction. That way you get to live—for a while, anyway."

"I could ask for a truthscope," Maro said. "I could lay this out for them."

The masked man laughed. "Who do you think would be running the 'scope? We own the brain scramblers on this planet. We own *lots* of things on this planet. You'd be better off to keep your mouth and mind shut, Maro, and take your loss gracefully. The Corporation would prefer that its name not come up, if you copy my meaning?"

Maro slumped back into his chair. They had him. They'd gone to a lot of trouble to get him, and he felt the power of it all around him. "Yeah. I copy."

The skinmask smiled. "Good. Nice to do business with a reasonable man. And nothing personal, you understand?"

"Sure. Nothing personal."

"Fine. You can get up. Get up. Get up. Get up . . ."

"—get up!"

Maro came out of the dream sweating. For a beat, he didn't know where he was—then it came back all too quickly.

A guard stood at the door to his cell, a big man who, from the look of the muscles swelling his uniform orthoskins, had spent more than a little time on a heavy-gee world. He had a face that practically radiated hate, deepset eyes under thick blond eyebrows, and a sneer that showed several perfect teeth.

The dream was the same as the memory, and he'd revisited both dozens of times in the last three months. Better, he knew, to face up to this unpleasant present than to dwell in the unchangeable past.

"They call me Lepto, when they speak to me," the

guard said. "And they don't speak unless I give them leave. You understand what I am telling you here?"

Maro nodded.

"That's good, fresh meat. Come on. We're going to the yard, you and me, and I am going to see how much they chew on you out there before I pull them off. You give me a good show, meat, and I don't let them kill you. You curl up too quick, and maybe I kill you myself. You understand what I am telling you here?"

"I understand."

"Good. Let's go."

The augmented image of Karnaaj peered at Stark from the video transceiver. White Radio did not transmit in color, for technical reasons having to do with FTL pulsations that Stark did not understand, but color was added on either end by computer. Sometimes, however, the computer enhancement seemed to be a little off, giving the subject a dead tone, as if the skin were lacking blood. With Karnaaj, the image always seemed to be that way, no matter what the computer did.

The voice came across fifteen light years. "I shall arrive there in three weeks," Karnaaj said. "Keep Maro alive until then. I would prefer that he be in a . . . receptive mood when I question him."

Stark stared at the Confed agent. He hated the man instinctively, but was careful not to let any of that show. "In other words, you want me to soften him up."

"Just so. But be warned. According to our psychological records, he has some kind of mind control technique that renders him immune to many forms of persuasion. He studied with some religious group called the Soul Melders for a time. Breaking him could be tricky. A wrong move and he might be lost to us. We would not want that."

"Of course not," Stark said.

"I see we understand one another."

Oh, I understand you well enough, Stark thought. *You are worse by far than most of the scum behind my walls.* Aloud, he said, "Yes."

"Then I shall see you in three weeks. Discom, Commander."

Stark did not reply, but reached up and waved the unit to darkness. He swiveled in his chair and stared out at the yard; then, abruptly, he turned back and touched a control on his com unit, set flush into the top of his desk. After a moment, Lepto's voice grated over it.

"Yessir?"

"Make sure that the prisoner Maro is able to leave the yard under his own power after the initiation. We have been ordered to keep him in one piece."

"Yessir." Lepto sounded disappointed.

Stark looked past the desk to the far wall of his office. Juete, still naked, lay sleeping on the couch. She might be tired, but it wasn't from their lovemaking, he knew. She could exhaust him totally and still have more energy than he'd had when they began. There was so much about her he didn't know, and so much he wanted to learn. She was a prisoner—guilty, like so many others in the Cage, of murder—but she was different, ah, so different! For, despite himself and his knowledge of the magic her pheromones worked, Stark loved the albino Exotic. It was more than sex, he was sure of that. He wanted to do things for her, to take care of her. When and if he ever left Omega, she would be going with him. He'd already had her sentence commuted, even though she was unaware of it. That had cost him, both in money and in favors, but it had been done. Only a few people knew of it, aside from himself, and no one inside the Cage.

As he watched the sleeping woman, he thought about Karnaaj's impending visit. That man could cause a lot of trouble. He would have to see what he could do to make

Maro more pliable; however, from their first meeting, Stark did not think that would be a particularly easy task. It didn't matter if it were easy or hard, though. He would do it.

One way or another.

* four *

Although Maro had never done any hard time—only short stretches in local locks—he knew people who had spent large portions of their lives in major prisons. He had heard the stories, some true, some apocryphal, and he had an idea of what his first visit to the yard might be like. It was there that a man's measure was taken. Or, as in the case of a cosexual and cospecies prison like the Cage, it was where a woman or muc would be sized up. It was an old game, barely civilized; an initiation, ofttimes brutal, into the pecking order.

As Maro walked into the yard, followed by the giant guard Lepto, he saw the sideways looks and quick glances that came from the prisoners. He took a deep breath. This wasn't going to be fun, but he knew that his status from here on would depend on how he acted and reacted.

"This is the yard," Lepto said. "Good luck." Then he turned and lumbered off.

There were a lot of ways he could play it, Maro knew. He could approach somebody and start a conversation. Or he could keep moving, to discourage someone else from doing the same. Perhaps he could find a corner and so protect his back. Or maybe he should just stand where he was and wait. In the long run, it probably wouldn't make much difference.

He decided on the latter course. Whatever procedure the inmates had devised for checking out new meat would swing into action no matter what he did, so there was no sense in delaying the inevitable.

Maro looked around. To his left, a group of five men stood around an old-style weight bench, watching. A woman, not particularly large but extremely well muscled, lay on her back upon the bench. She wore a pair of shorts, a halter, and half-fingered lifting gloves. Across the supports was a bar loaded with steel plates. This was a one-gee world, or thereabouts, and Maro quickly estimated the amount of weight stacked on the bar. It looked to be about a hundred and ninety kilos, counting the bar itself. His eyebrows went up slightly. He *might* be able to bench that much, if his life depended on it. Then again, the woman looked like she weighed no more than sixty kilos, which made the amount of iron she was working with more than three times her own bodyweight. That would put her in world-class range on most worlds, for men or women. He doubted she would be able to get steroids in the Cage, and that made it even more impressive.

As he watched, the woman gripped the bar, lifted it from the supports without any of the watchers spotting her, and proceeded to bench press the weight eight times in a smooth, easy motion.

Maro turned away. If she was doing reps with that much, it was likely she could push a lot more for a single or double. Which made her stronger than just about anyone he had ever seen; certainly much stronger than he was.

Behind him, a voice said, "The woman you've been admiring is called Raze. She's from Tatsu, just like Lepto. It's a heavy-gravity world."

Maro turned slowly to see a short, slightly built man of about forty-five T.S., with a professorial air. The left side of his head was permanently depilated, and he wore a flat-pack droud plugged into an inset skull socket.

"They call me Scanner," the man said, raising a hand in a palm-out greeting. Maro returned the gesture. "Dain Maro." He looked back at Raze, who was now on her third set. A light sheen of perspiration coated her skin, and the muscles were pumped to an impressive degree.

"High-gee or not," he said, "she's strong." He looked back at Scanner. "A mue?"

Scanner looked back at Raze and smiled slightly. "Not exactly, though she's had a few genes spliced. But the primary trick is forced superdense musculature growth, alloy-reinforced bone structure, and nylon ligaments. She can probably punch through steel." He paused, then said, "Our psychopathic friend who brought you out here would like very much to have carnal knowledge of Raze. But the warden doesn't like fraternization. Except, of course, for Juete and him."

Juete . . . "The albino."

"You saw her?"

Maro nodded. "I saw her."

Scanner laughed. "She's an Exotic, from the Darkworld. Genetic playtoys, originally, but they bred true. Pheromonically potent and designed to attract anything remotely human, male or female. You felt her pull, I take it?"

"I felt it."

The small man laughed again. "Oh, yeah, everybody who gets close to Juete feels it. But she's the warden's property, top to bottom. Lay a hand on her and you're dead. Believe me, more than a few have tried."

Maro was about to reply, when suddenly there was a shriek like torn metal, and a batwinged shadow blotted out the sun. Scanner hurled himself toward Maro, knocking the smuggler off his feet. "Get down!" he shouted.

Maro rolled over and looked up, shielding his eyes against the sun. He had a confused impression of something banking and diving toward him with the sun at its back, something huge, with leathery, claw-tipped wings and a giant hammerhead split with gleaming teeth. Then it was past him and arrowing toward the weightlifter.

Maro saw Raze, now off the bench and standing amidst a pile of iron plates and other weightlifting paraphernalia. The other prisoners who had been watching her scattered as the flying predator dove toward her. Raze, however, didn't run—instead she grabbed a five-kilo plate and hurled it like a discus at the thing swooping toward her. The plate struck the creature in the head, and with another shriek, this time of anger and pain, it swerved away.

Maro got to his feet, still bewildered by the swiftness of it all. Around him, other prisoners were rising also. They immediately resumed whatever it was they had been doing before the attack. No one showed much surprise or reaction. Maro looked questioningly at Scanner.

"Dragonbat," Scanner said. "One of Omega's larger and more unfriendly lifeforms. Every now and then they like to drop into the yard for a snack."

Maro looked at the towers, where the guards were grinning as they watched the prisoners. He heard Scanner add, "The guards' weapons always seem to be out of ammo when it happens."

He looked back at Raze, who had calmly resumed her workout. "Looks like it picked the wrong meal this time," he said.

Then he felt a cold chill run up his spine as Scanner said, too casually, "Someone's coming to do you."

That confirmed what Maro had anticipated. Somebody would be testing him. He relaxed, his senses alert, waiting for whatever form the attack would take—

"Well. What have we here?"

Maro turned slightly to view the speaker. He did not let his surprise show; if anything, the man was even more innocuous-looking than Scanner. He wasn't a dwarf, but he wasn't much larger. And he had the face of a saint—smooth skin, no wrinkles except deep laugh lines, and electric green eyes. The snide voice didn't go at all with the face. Maro couldn't figure out how old the man was; he could be anywhere from twenty to forty. He was sure, however, that the saintly appearance was misleading. Looking like he did and still being alive in the Cage, he had to have something going for him. Some kind of martial art, perhaps?

"What a sweet ass you have," the saint said. "I'll just have me a piece of it."

Maro tensed. Rape in a crowded prison yard didn't seem likely, not with guards watching. But *something* was going to happen . . . He couldn't stop looking at the man's eyes. They were so green that they seemed to glow, to expand somehow, filling his vision . . .

And suddenly, with no sense of transition whatsoever, he was no longer in the yard. He was in a seraglio—a huge chamber with satin wall hangings. He was nude and chained face down on a large bed covered with black silk sheets. He twisted his head, and could just glimpse the dwarf standing behind him. He was wearing leather trappings and robes now. He stood behind the bed, chuckling, and parted the robes slowly to reveal an enormous erection.

Maro struggled, but the chains held him firmly. His mind was dazed—where was he, and how had he gotten here?

It's not real, *he thought, and suddenly knew that was the truth of it. Maro took a deep breath and let it slowly escape, then began to set his mind in the Defense Cast he had learned from the Soul Melders—*

The dwarf's laughter grew louder and louder. Maro could feel the man touching him, stroking him lasciviously. He forced himself to divorce himself from the feelings of revulsion and outrage, to reach within himself for the strength necessary to fight . . .

And then, just as suddenly as before, he was back in the yard. He staggered backward as though he had just broken free of a tether. He could feel sweat running down his face. The dwarf had not moved, but there was a look of shock on his face. Then, as Maro regained his balance and stepped forward again, the shock was replaced with fear. The dwarf turned and ran.

Maro saw Scanner and some of the other inmates looking at him with new-found respect.

"Amazing. Nobody ever did that to the Mindfucker before," Scanner said softly. "He's one of the strongest empaths in the galaxy."

Maro turned slightly to look at the other man. "Is this it?"

Scanner shook his head. "One more. Sandoz."

"More mind games?"

"No. Sandoz is nothing if not physical."

Maro spun in a small circle, searching the yard, feeling for danger, looking for someone who carried himself or herself in a way that suggested more than usual competence. He was fairly good with his hands and feet—close combat was taught by the Melders as part of body control—but he wasn't good enough to do more than slow a real expert, without surprise on his side. But they had also taught him how to recognize a real expert. Look for balance, for centeredness, for confidence, open your senses and feel the *ki*. You can sense it, if it is powerful enough.

There. There he was. A tall man, well-built but not like a bodybuilder, looking away from Maro.

Maro walked toward the man, stopping three meters away. The other still had his back to Maro, but there was no doubt that he was aware of the smuggler.

Maro took a deep breath. "Let's get it over with," he said.

The other man turned as if surprised. He had ordinary features, was, in fact, so average in appearance that Maro felt he could blend into a crowd of two and be anonymous. He raised an eyebrow, then shifted his feet by maybe two centimeters.

There was only one way he could survive this, Maro knew. He had to balance the other man's movements perfectly. The slightest misalignment would be fatal. This man was *dangerous*. He moved his own stance a hair, trying to stay tuned to the other's energies.

Sandoz leaned, hardly a motion at all.

Maro took a half step to his left.

Sandoz grinned, as if to say, Hey, someone who knows how to play. He backed up six centimeters and twisted slightly to his right—and Maro lost the thread that connected them. He moved forward and slightly aslant to the right, realized his error, and compensated by quickly sliding to the left. The balance was struck again, but—

"Slow," Sandoz said. "I could have taken you."

"Yes," Maro said.

"But not bad. You get points for recognizing me, and points for two out of three." He grinned again. "And we both know how it would have gone—right?"

"We know," Maro said. The man could have killed him with no effort, had he chosen to do so. He was better than anybody Maro had ever faced, and that included his instructors.

Sandoz extended his palm. "Welcome to the Cage," he said.

Maro blew out his breath in a sigh. He had just passed the initiation and was alive to celebrate.

Lepto's voice on Stark's com sounded very unhappy. Stark was more than a little amazed to hear what the guard had to say.

"—nothing happened. I mean *nothing*, do you understand what I am telling you here? First the pervert bracketed him, then next thing you know the little turd was running away. This Maro, he never even moved, never touched the guy."

"I see," Stark said. "And Sandoz?"

"That was even weirder. He had maybe two words with Scanner and then stalked off to bracket Sandoz." Lepto paused there. Stark was surprised; *nobody* stalked Sandoz. As a personal assassin, he was second to no one in the cage. Aside from contract killing, he had walked the Musashi Flex, for *fun*. Never defeated there, and never missed a paid snuff. They would never have caught him, either, if a nervous client hadn't turned him in. Even Lepto, who feared no one else, stayed calm around Sandoz.

"He and Sandoz shuffled around for a few minutes like a couple of old maids on a dance floor, then all of a sudden they were pals. I don't copy it, Warden. This guy's got something strange working."

Indeed, Stark thought. But he did not say so. Instead, he merely said, "It doesn't matter. The Confed wants him. When they're done with him, I doubt he'll have much of anything left working."

"Yeah, right," Lepto said. He didn't hide the glee in his voice.

Stark shook his head in disgust. Lepto was a sociopath. Useful, but a star on the edge of going nova. Stark didn't want to be anywhere close when Lepto finally let go.

"It doesn't seem as though he's in any danger from the yard scum, not if Sandoz likes him. Keep a long eye on him, but otherwise leave him alone."

"Copy that, Warden."

"Discom," Stark said.

He leaned back in the chair and stared at the ceiling, his fingers steepled. Interesting. Another time, another place, and maybe Maro would have been somebody worth getting to know. But not here and now. Now, the man was just another number, another member of the herd of animals he had to control. He felt a vague regret, but he quickly shunted it aside. Things were as they were. And, mind control or not, Maro would soon be only a walking shell, after the Confed got through with him.

* five *

As the sun climbed higher, the heat grew more oppressive. When Maro had first arrived in the yard, it had been early enough to be hot, but not too bad. Now the day felt tropical. Sweat ran and stained his coverall, and if there was any evaporation, he did not notice it. The humidity must be almost a hundred percent, the temperature close to body heat.

Scanner was introducing Maro to other prisoners and giving him a basic outline of operations inside the Cage.

"No rehab, of course," Scanner said. "Nobody leaves, so why bother? There is some work to be done, mostly seasonal. We have to be pretty much self-sufficient. We grow our own food, mostly, and do all of the construction work ourselves. What has to be imported costs, and the Confed doesn't see wasting a lot of stads on us."

Raze came up to them. Maro waited for Scanner to finish his short speech, then nodded once at the woman. She was shorter than Maro by five centimeters, and by this time had worked up a bright sheen of sweat. The thin shorts and halter were plastered to her, and despite the play of muscles under her tanned skin, there was no doubt whatsoever that she was female. She smiled at him.

"Nice move on the Mindfucker," she said. "He did me when I got here and it wasn't fun."

"What did you do afterward?" Maro asked.

She shrugged. "Came up behind the little bastard and broke his arm. He doesn't bother me now."

I'll bet, Maro thought. *I'd bet nobody bothers you much.*

"Got to finish my last set of squats. See you later." Raze drifted away.

"This is Chameleon," Scanner said, gesturing to a short, bearded man walking toward them. To him, Scanner said, "How do you stand the heat with that beard?"

Chameleon smiled. "You've got a point." As Maro watched in astonishment, the beard seemed to fade, grow lighter, and start to disappear. He realized that the hair was being *absorbed* back into the skin. After five seconds it was gone. And more—Chameleon's skin darkened from a medium tan to a dark brown. It was like watching a sun-sensor plate react to light.

Scanner, grinning, said, "Chameleon is from Raft. Before the Interdiction they did some interesting experimental genetic work there. Some of it stayed viable, some not. About one in ten thousand Raftians can do his tricks."

"Only about one in a million's got my kinda control, though," Chameleon said. "I can make all *kinds* of things change."

Scanner laughed. "Chameleon is in for sex crimes," he said to Maro.

"A drop-shot! I was innocent!"

"The ladies loved him, but their fathers, brothers, and spouses didn't. He got too close to a Confed hiwate's daughter."

"She didn't complain."

"She was underage, wasn't she?"

"Six friggin' months! You can't put a limit on love, now can you?"

"The Confed can," Scanner said.

They moved away, leaving Chameleon to ponder his memories.

"Over there, that skinny guy, that's Fish. He's crazy. Holds the record for murders, if you count long distance and not face-to-face."

"What did he do?"

"Torpedoed an intersystem shuttle just to watch the people die of explosive decompression. Six thousand, including the ones in the bomb-rigged lifepods. He recorded it all on spheres. Still carries them—see the little steel marbles he's fiddling with? He's what they call a muerte-orgasmic; he gets off on death."

"How about the fat man, there?" Maro asked. "Next to the wall, in the shade."

"Ah, that's Berque. A slaver and organrunner. Ran a meat market on one of the wheelworlds, Jicha Mungo, I think, in the Bibi Arusi System. Bought and sold men, women, children, mues, standards—you name it. He's had a full round of implants himself: new liver, heart, lungs, spleen, kidneys, eyes, testicles. I understand he also developed a taste for long pig. His own best customer, before they caught up to him."

"Nice," Maro said.

"Yeah, don't say anything to him that you want kept secret from the warden. We're fairly sure he's a dip for the guards, but we can't pin him."

"A lot of fun people here," Maro observed.

Scanner laughed again. His voice took on a mock serious tone: "Yeah, this place is full of criminals!"

"What about you, Scanner. Can I ask?"

"Sure. I'm a circuit-rider; I do the electron dance. Sometimes you can get real deep into systems; you find out things you didn't want to know. Everybody's got secrets, and some of the worst ones belong to those with the most power. The only reason I'm alive is they know that when I die a White Radio relay clicks shut and some of those secrets get transferred to public places. But they want me out of the way until they can figure a way to dig out what I know and wipe it clean.''

''Nothing more than that?''

Scanner grinned again, and tapped the droud. ''Well, I also stole a few million standards here and there.''

Maro returned the grin. He liked Scanner; the man had a lot of rogue in him, just like his old mentor Vickers.

The two of them moved toward the hard shade; the sun was too hot to endure any longer. Over near one wall Maro noted a small group of people—even through the shimmer of heat waves from the packed dirt he could see that their skins were covered with scales.

Scanner noticed the direction of his gaze and said, ''You'll want to watch out for the mue gangs. Probably they won't bother you once word gets out that you're tight with Sandoz, but accidents happen. They don't much like standard terran stock. There are three main gangs: the Wets, from Aqua; the Squats, from Vishnu; and the Scales, from Pentr'ado. The Scales are the worst, so stay clear if you see more than two of them together. They have a taste for blood, literally, and a couple of guys have been found real dry after a round with them.''

''I'll remember,'' Maro said.

Standing in the shade helped somewhat, but it was still hot. The air was unstirred by any breeze, and there was little movement from the inmates as the sun passed directly overhead. Mostly everybody stood around marking time until it got cooler. There were perhaps three hundred men and women in the yard, and, according to Scanner, twice that many more doing work or freetime elsewhere in and around the prison. Fewer than a thousand souls, held in check by about a hundred guards. But those guards were well-armed and brutal, and led by a warden who had, according to Scanner, been responsible for the deaths of more than six dozen inmates in the last year.

It was a good place to leave in a hurry, Maro thought. As soon as he could figure out how, he was gone.

The sunlight dimmed. He glanced up in relief, only to see dark, angry clouds massing overhead. He felt a splash of warm water on his neck. It was beginning to rain.

The new cooler arrived, and Stark inspected it as the technician stripped the packing away. A heavier model, this one, designed for tropical use, or so it was advertised. Once activated it would follow him any time he went outside, circulating streams of cool air around him in an attempt to combat the incessant heat. He could, he supposed, have bought a climatesuit, but they were bulky, expensive, and prone to malfunction even more so than coolers. No, the cooler would work well enough. And this one had an umbrella field built in that could be polarized to keep out both light and rain.

Speaking of which, it was beginning to come down again. Tropical thunderstorms were fierce on Omega, at least in this latitude. An afternoon downpour could drop eight centimeters of warm rain, blow down two or three trees, and make the lightning arrestors dance, then wash away and leave the prison nearly as hot as before. He hated this place.

Juete drifted into the supply room and stood watching the cooler being unpacked. It was more for her than himself that he had ordered the machine; she could not spend much time outside, even slathered in sunblock and with dark contacts. The Exotics had been designed as inside toys and bred for life on a world where the sun only shone a short time each year. Omega was a textbook definition of hell for her. She did not sweat much, her glands were modified, and so she could keel over with heatstroke if not protected properly. The cooler would also be adapted to follow her.

He gestured at it. "It's for you."

She stared at the unit, not speaking, and once more Stark felt that stab of disappointment. If only she could see how much he cared for her! Well, she would someday. After all, he had the rest of her life.

"This is the best prison food I have ever tasted," Maro said. "In fact, it might be some of the best food I've ever had anywhere."

Across the table from him, Scanner smiled. "One of the joys of being on a backward world. We grow our own, so it's fresh, clean, and cheap. Those carrots are completely organic, and the fruit so abundant that most of it rots before we can get to it."

Maro took another bite of the thick, black bread and washed it down with cold water from the metal cup. "A meal like this would cost a week's pay in most ports."

"I guess they figure it's better to keep us fat and happy than lean and hungry."

Maro finished a mouthful of carrots before he spoke again. "So," he asked casually, "who has plans to escape in the works?"

Scanner almost choked on his water. "Escape?" he finally managed. "Nobody. Didn't you get the warden's speech when you arrived? We are null for null here. Nobody has ever escaped from the Omega Cage."

"There's always a first time," Maro replied.

Scanner shook his head. "You are wasting your time, Dain. You saw what happened to the last six who tried it."

"So you plan to stay here for the rest of your life?"

"At least I'm alive."

"So am I. And I plan to stay alive for a long time after I'm gone from here."

Scanner shrugged. "You won't get much help. The only ones who try it are crazy—everybody knows that."

"*I* don't know it."

"Maybe we can convince you."

Maro smiled. "Maybe. And maybe I can convince *you*."

In the yard, the lasts vestiges of the afternoon's rainstorm played over the thick grass and dirt, adding final drops to ankle-deep puddles. The thunder moved further away, becoming only a distant echo, and the lightning was now only a faint and occasional flash.

Maro stood under the overhang of the tool shed next to Scanner; Raze leaned against the rough-cut wood, doing fingertip presses—using one finger on each hand in quick rotations. A man called Patch stood with his back to the dying rain. He had both eyes; he got his name from a squarish birthmark that covered half his face. Apparently plastic surgery hadn't advanced very far on his homeworld.

"Suppose you did manage to get past the wall," Patch said. "Then what? There are only two spaceports on this world. The closest is a thousand klicks away—the other one is twice that far."

"That's not so far—" Maro began.

"No, not on Earth or Shin or Koji, maybe. But there's nothing on this world that likes humans, except maybe to eat them. If it walks, slithers, crawls or flies, if it carries poison or has teeth, it probably lives on this stinking planet."

"So it won't be easy," Maro said. "I never said it would."

Sandoz laughed. "Once I went up against three of the Confed's crack combat troopers. These three were all in the same squad, trained to kill at the drop of a slipper, and circulating bacteria-aug for speed. I just barely survived the encounter. *That* was easy compared to getting out of here." He looked at Scanner. "Give him the numbers."

Scanner said, "In the sixty-nine years since the prison opened there have been five hundred and twelve attempted escapes from the Omega Cage. Of that number, three hundred and eighty-seven escapees were killed outright; one hundred and two subsequently died from injuries received while attempting escape; and twenty-three were recaptured without fatal wounds. Of the twenty-three prisoners recaptured, seventeen died while undergoing punitive treatment; two committed suicide; and three were killed by a person or persons unknown."

Maro did some quick mental arithmetic. "That leaves one. What happened to him?"

"Right here," Sandoz said. "I survived a year in the Pit and four guard-sponsored hitters."

"What happened to them? The ones who tried to kill you?"

Sandoz grinned. "What do you think?"

"So you've decided the risk isn't worth it?"

The assassin looked at Maro squarely. "I didn't say that. I said it would be hard. I wanted you to know."

Maro grinned. "Okay, so now I know. I want *you* to understand that I am going to find a way out. I don't have a plan yet, but I'll get to that. I have some experience in this line of work. There is *always* a way out. Just because nobody has ever done it before doesn't mean no one can ever do it."

Raze finished her fingertip exercises and turned to face Maro. "You work it up, Maro, and let me know what you want me to do. I'd rather die out there than live forever in here."

Maro looked around at the others. Silently, they all nodded.

He took a deep breath. He had a team. Now all he had to do was come up with a way.

* six *

After hearing about Maro's sailing through the normally deadly initiation of new prisoners, Stark had a feeling that softening the smuggler up prior to his interrogation by Karnaaj might not be that easy. The usual methods lacked sufficient power, that seemed obvious enough. Ordinary threats seldom bothered full-termers; drugs or induced hypnogogia seemed contraindicated; physical torture without the proper monitoring gear entailed risk. Fear, as always, was the key, but how to invoke it in Maro?

Stark nodded to the tech running the mindwipe machineries. The woman returned the nod, then went back to tuning the equipment. The room was small, hardly large enough for the chair bolted to the floor in the center. There wasn't need for much room, however, since the audience stood or sat in a separate chamber, along with the electronics used to run the chair.

Stark stared at the chair. Maro was a disciple of some kind of mind control; he had proved that by defeating the perverted telepath known as the Mindfucker. It seemed logical to assume that Maro would have spent a lot of time working on his thought processes, on exploration of his own psyche. Therefore, it might be that his fears would lie in that area; perhaps keeping his mind sacrosanct was more important than keeping his physical body intact.

He could not be exposed to mindwipe, of course—not until Karnaaj had had his way with him—but perhaps the threat of it might agitate Maro somewhat. It was worth a try.

"We're almost ready," the tech said.

"Good." The warden turned away and touched the compatch on his throat. "Bring Maro to the Psychiatric Implimentorium."

Lepto strolled across the yard, swaggering somewhat as he passed Raze. Raze, in the middle of curling a heavy barbell, paused long enough to spit to one side as Lepto walked by. Her meaning was clear enough; the massive guard colored slightly and shortened his steps into a more military motion.

Maro watched the guard come and held his face as impassive as he could. To smile might be worth a visit to the dental clinic.

"The warden wants you," Lepto said.

Scanner whispered to Maro as Lepto turned away. "You're in for a visit to the Zombie Ward; I just got the word."

"How?" Maro whispered back.

Scanner touched his droud, then turned away as Lepto looked back. "*Now,*" Lepto said, his voice soft and dangerous.

Maro moved. He knew about the mindwipe process. Sometimes it was ordered as part of a convicted man's sentence; sometimes the authorities of a particular prison took it upon themselves to order the procedure on their own. On full-termers it was their option.

Maro felt a stab of cold fear as he followed the guard through the hot afternoon. If that was what was in store for him, he would try to meet it calmly, but he was afraid he would lose that resolve when it came down to it. He had an option: part of his training had included a method of triggering the *R*-complex, the reptilian hindbrain that controlled the autonomic functions in everyone, into shutdown. If worse came to worst, he could kill himself before his psyche was shattered. Better to die whole than to live as a vegetable.

But better by far to live whole than either of the other options, said a little voice inside his head. *Give them whatever they want.*

Inside the chamber, a big man sat in the chair. There seemed to be no restraints holding him in place, nor any electronic connections, but the strain on his body showed in the tension of his muscles. He was trying to move and could not, that was apparent.

"Stasis field," the warden said, smiling at Maro. "And the electronics are all induced. Listen." Stark waved one hand, and the sound of the prisoner in the chair reached Maro's ears, amplified for clarity.

"—fuck you, all of you, I spit on you—!"

The warden waved his hand again and the volume of the prisoner's curses fell sharply, becoming a tinny whine.

"You're looking at a man who refuses to get along with the universe," the warden said. "A killer, of course; that wouldn't set him apart in here, but he's one who took particular joy in it. Still, others in the Cage could claim that distinction as well."

Maro couldn't help himself. He asked, "Then why this?"

Stark grinned wolfishly. "He killed a guard. One of my men. The guard in question was gutter scum, hardly better than most of you inmates. But he was one of *mine*."

Maro turned back to watch the struggling man. *Of course.*

"Go," Stark said to the technician.

The woman adjusted several controls on her board. The cursing stopped as if cut off by a knife. "Mom?" the prisoner said.

"Early memories first," Stark murmured.

"Oh, baby, yeah, just like that!"

"And the ones with the greatest emotional attachment seem to clear fastest," the warden continued, as if discussing the weather.

In the chair, the man smiled beatifically.

"Probably a killing," Stark said. "An early one, when it was still fun for him."

Maro watched as emotions danced across the prisoner's face. He smiled, cried, laughed, gritted his teeth, gasped, and screamed. What was so horrible about it was that he did each thing so quickly, shifting from expression to expression as if each was meaningless. Maro would not have believed that such an emotional range at that speed was possible.

It took only five minutes. In the end, the man sat with as neutral a face as that of a life-sized doll.

"Let's call him, oh, how about . . . Dain?" the warden said.

Maro turned to stare at Stark.

"What his name was doesn't matter; he won't answer to it now. He doesn't remember it—or anything else. Oh, he'll be reeducated—we have some viral programs we can infect him with that will give him basic skills. He'll be able to feed himself and defecate in a toilet, and he'll have a basic command of language. Then our new Dain will be a useful member of our little society. He can spend the rest of his days working happily at some simple job such as peeling vegetables or pulling weeds, and never have a worry past that. Of course, he won't remember anything about who he was, but that's not all that important, is it?"

Maro did not trust himself to speak. He had a sudden urge to throttle the warden, to choke him until he gasped for breath and turned blue. He clenched his fists to control himself. *Easy, Dain.* He knew Stark had some reason for showing him this. He wouldn't let the man's sadistic little show get to him.

"Perhaps you're wondering why I arranged this little entertainment," Stark said. "Quite simple, really. You need to know what happens to people who don't cooperate with us."

"So now I know," Maro said.

"Oh, yes. Now you know."

In the yard, Scanner was puzzled. "Nobody ever got pulled to watch a wipe before, far as I know. There's something strange going on here."

Maro nodded at Scanner's droud. "Can you find out what?"

"Maybe. If I'm careful." Scanner shrugged. "Not for a few days, though. Our shift works the garden tomorrow."

"I ran a tractor when I was a kid," Maro said.

Scanner laughed. "Tractor? That won't come in very handy. Everything here is done the hard way. I hope you've had experience with a rake or a hoe."

"You're joking. Even the most backward world—"

"—has machinery," Scanner finished. "But this is Omega, remember? We're not just backward—we're last."

"I guess so."

Scanner grinned. "Cheer up—at least you get to see outside. You'll find it interesting, I assure you."

With the dawn, Maro was awakened by a clanging gong. He was hastily herded into formation along with a hundred other prisoners, marched through the main ground gate and along a rutted dirt road for a half-klick to the west end of the Zonn wall. Ten guards, armed with laser-aimed automatic shotguns, rode along with them in three small, wheeled electric trucks.

As they marched, Maro asked Scanner, "There many of those vehicles around?"

"Maybe a dozen, but forget it. Nothing that moves on the ground would get more than a few klicks away. There are no roads except the ones right around the prison. Between the swamps and the deserts, a truck would be about as useful as a pseudopod."

Something screamed then, an inhuman howl of rage. Maro twisted just in time to see a four-legged beast the size of a big dog charging from a thick stand of brush directly at the line of prisoners. A dot of red light appeared on the thing's fur suddenly, and then the shotguns went off. One of the guards near Maro had jumped from the truck and now stood wide-legged, his weapon held at hip level, firing on full auto. The roar was continuous.

The dog-beast stopped as if it had run into a solid wall. Blood gouted from its fur and its snout and eyes vanished as if wiped away by a steel claw. Several shotgun blasts had connected, and in an instant the thing was nothing more than a mass of red fur and gore.

After the shotguns blasts, the silence seemed all the more deadly.

Maro looked questioningly at Scanner. "Bush dog," the latter said. "Nasty critters—not scared of anything. The jungle is full of them. Also full of snakes, *T*-birds, dragonbats, creepers, suck vines and shrats—that's what they call a little beast the size of a rabbit that looks like a cross between a shrew and a rat. Meaner than a wolverine. Then there's the insects, spiders and poison thorns. Something to think about, my friend. The guns and guards aren't to keep us from running when we're in the field; they're to protect us. On a good day we'll get maybe half a dozen bush dogs attacking, as well as some *T*-birds—*T* as in teeth—a dragonbat or two, and the shrats."

"You're serious," Maro said.

"Oh, yeah. The plants you don't have to worry about

much—we're working in a cleared area—and the bugs are kept down by low-voltage zap fields. But the animals don't have enough sense to be afraid. I watched a pack of dogs come at us one at a time, once. Each one watched the one in front of it get blown away, and yet each one made his run."

"This doesn't sound promising."

Scanner grinned. "Now you see a little more clearly why there hasn't been a general exodus of prisoners seeking their fortunes in the hospitable Omegan landscape?"

Maro exhaled. "Yeah."

Juete massaged his naked back as Stark lay face down on his bed. She straddled his hips, leaning into the motions, the heels of her hands pressing hard against the knots in his muscles. She was very good at this; of course, Exotics were taught such things almost from birth. He felt the tension begin to ebb.

"I think I'm going to have trouble with the new inmate," Stark said into the pillow under his head. Even though he lay nude upon the sheet, the chill of the air conditioner barely kept him cool.

"Oh?" her voice was noncommittal. Polite interest, no more.

"He knows something that the Confed wants. Something about Black Sun. They're sending one of the *Soldatutmarkt* ghouls to question him personally. A man named Karnaaj."

The rhythm of her hands faltered for a moment, then resumed.

"Something wrong?"

Juete changed into a percussive mode, pounding along the sides of his spine. "I—think I have heard the name." The hammering of her small fists felt wonderful.

"Karnaaj is not a nice man. Maro will find that out."

Abruptly he twisted, so that he now lay on his back.

Juete now straddled his crotch. She was as naked as he was. "'Come here,'' he commanded, pulling her down to his chest. He thrust and slid easily into her. She was ready. She was always ready.

To hell with Maro. To hell with Karnaaj. This was all that was important, to be with this woman, to be in her and moving this way. Juete moaned and began moving faster. Stark grinned fiercely at the ceiling. As grim and horrible as Omega was, this was *his* world. He would let no one interfere with the way he ran it—not even the Confed.

✳ seven ✳

After two days of broiling in the tropical sunshine and fending off an amazing number of attacks by Omega's native flora and fauna, Maro's shift was relieved of garden chores. The next duty would be spent cleaning and painting inside the prison, an easier job by far. When the third day began, Maro found himself at work in the miniscule library, along with Scanner, restocking shelves.

"I pulled in a couple of favors for this duty," Scanner said in a low tone, watching the guard amble away from them. "Watch the portal."

Maro did as he was instructed. The hallway outside was empty. He said as much.

"Good. Let me know if that changes."

Scanner went to a shelf of old-style video cartridges. From one of the plastic units he removed a small object, which he held up for Maro to see. It took a moment for the smuggler to realize what it was: a droud plug of some kind.

The electronics master moved to the library's computer console, keyed in a sequence, then sat down in the chair before the blank screen. He then inserted the droud plug into his skull socket. The other end of the cable he jacked into one of the computer's ports. His face immediately cleared of expression; he looked, Maro thought, much as the mindwiped prisoner had looked after the procedure that had taken his identity.

Maro stared at his friend for a moment, then glanced back out into the hallway. Still empty.

Thirty seconds passed.

"That's it," Scanner said.

Maro turned to see the smaller man disconnecting the droud plug. "Fast," Maro said.

Scanner smiled. "Slow. I just spent the equivalent of a long vacation browsing the prison computer's files on you. And I'm sorry to say that you are up to your armpits in excrement, friend."

Stark stood on the balcony outside his personal cube, watching a line of men dig a trench for new water piping. Next to him the portable cooler hummed, setting a convection current of cold air swirling around him, protection against the heat of the day.

Stark felt uneasy, though he could not have said exactly why. There was no reason for it. The prisoners were quiet enough; the assigned work was either on time or actually ahead of schedule; he had just been with Juete and was sated. And yet something prodded him, a nagging itch at the edges of his perception.

He turned away irritably from the digging men and moved to the other end of the balcony. The cooler followed him, doglike, its tone changing as it sped up to chill the additional hot air.

Maybe it was the impending visit by Karnaaj. A few more days and the man would be here. Ostensibly, Karnaaj had no direct power over him; practically, a bad report from the man would weigh heavily upon Stark. A smooth-working prison had to greet the Confed man, and it seemed almost too good to be true that things were going so well currently. He worried that it might be the calm before the storm. He most assuredly did not wish for any disturbance while Karnaaj was within earshot.

He would have his guards pay special attention to the day-to-day operations, and his dips among the prisoners would be told to bring rumors of anything as soon as they heard them. If this were a prison on any civilized world he would have a bevy of electronics eavesdropping everywhere. Every grunt would register, be computer analyzed and extrapolated for meaning—if he had the equipment. *Might as well wish for a billion standards, tax free, while you are at it,* Stark told himself sarcastically. He didn't have the gear or the budget for it. In many ways—most ways—his operation here was no better off than one of the many penitentiaries on Earth centuries ago. There was no help for that; he would simply have to make do.

Well, that wasn't strictly true. There were some items he had managed to secure either by favors or more devious means. If things ever got really bad he had the Juggernaut . . .

Stark turned back toward his cube. No point in worrying about worst-case scenarios; they weren't likely to happen. No, he just had to keep things running smoothly until Karnaaj sucked Maro dry and left. After that, things would be back to normal.

Or as normal as they got around here . . .

Supper done, Maro moved to the yard. Insects buzzed and fluttered, despite the small zap fields set up around the prison. The tropical night began to enshroud the yard, and fat moths came out to bounce from the big HT lamps that bathed the prison in hard-edged brightness.

He hated this time of day, no matter what world he was on. He hated it particularly if he was in a prison yard, because then it was most difficult to ignore the voices far at the back of his skull that reminded him of what his life had come to, what it might have been, had things gone differently . . .

"I hear you maybe have trouble on the way," a voice said behind him. It was Raze.

Without turning, Maro said, "Maybe."

"Karnaaj has been here before," she said. "Been a while. Last guy he came to see didn't survive it."

Maro turned slowly. The bodybuilder wore a prison coverall, opened enough so that he could see the tan lines on her body, pale against the darker brown overlaying the hard muscle.

"You know anything about Black Sun?" he asked.

Raze shrugged. "What everybody does. I never did much business with them directly."

"I did. As long as I did what they wanted, we got along. I was pretty good at my trade; I could get things on and off some tight planets. Black Sun contracted for my services more than a few times. Until I decided I could make a better profit on my own."

Raze smiled. "A mistake?"

Maro laughed, a short, bitter sound. "Some people might think so. I'm in here because I stepped on their toes. I never was very good at taking orders."

"You know a lot about them."

"So Scanner told you. Yes. And I figure Karnaaj plans to either score points by snapping up a few minor operators to dangle before his Confed bosses, or else buy his way into the organization, to cut a piece of the action."

"You gonna tell him what you know?"

A few more prisoners drifted toward them. Maro saw Scanner and Sandoz among the inmates.

"I think not."

Raze laughed, a pleasant sound. "Honor among thieves? Or are you worried that Black Sun will get to you even here?"

It was Maro's turn to shrug. "If they want me bad

enough, they could find me if I were hiding in a black hole. I don't owe them anything. Then again, I owe the Confed even less. Black Sun set me up, but the Confed runs this pit. Black Sun at least admits to what it is—criminals out to make a profit. The Confed pretends to be a benevolent government, which is as big a lie as ever was told in this galaxy. I'd rather be dead than help them."

"Nice speech," Sandoz said. "But how well do you think it'll work when they start hammering on you? You'll tell them then. You won't have a choice. They'll pry it out of you. I know—I've been there."

"At least they'll *have* to pry it out," Maro said.

"Maybe it won't come to that," Scanner murmured.

The others looked at him. He continued, "I found something else while I was dancing over your file. A map. Very detailed, covering the entire hemisphere. If you can figure a way to get us over the wall, I can plot a path away from here."

There was silence for a long moment. "Why didn't you find this before?" Sandoz asked suspiciously. "You've been poking around in that goddamned computer for five years."

Scanner shook his head. "I don't know. It wasn't there before."

"Could it be a trick? Put there for you to find?"

"I don't think so," Scanner said. "It shows things some of us have seen, just where they're supposed to be. I don't think they know I can get in. I don't leave tracks."

Maro said, "It's worth looking at, this map. If we can figure out a way over the wall . . ."

"That should be easy," Sandoz said, his voice heavy with irony.

Maro looked at Scanner. "You know anything about interparticle physics?"

Scanner gave out one short chuckle. "Oh, sure. Every night before I go to sleep I try to read all the latest sub-atomic research, done by my esteemed colleagues here." He waved one hand to encompass the other inmates.

Maro ignored the sarcasm. "You know what a Bender is?"

"I know that, yes."

"Can you find out about the Zonn? Anything on the city they left here?"

"I can find what there is," Scanner said. "Why?"

"Maybe nothing. But," Maro said, "I met a man once—a xenologist. He told me some things about the Zonn artifacts; some theories about the materials they used. It might help us."

Sandoz smiled. "I can tell you the stuff makes diamond look like clay. Half a million years old and there isn't a scratch on it. You planning on walking through those walls, Maro?"

Maro said, "I don't know. Maybe."

Juete lay next to Stark, listening to the even sound of the warden's breathing. He was asleep, but unless she moved with great care, she would awaken him. She could tell him she was going to the fresher, which was true enough; but if he were awake, he would wait for her to return. And likely he would want her again. As much as she liked sex, as much as she had to have it, she did not want to be with Stark right now. To be a prisoner was bad enough; to be a slave was worse. She hated him; worse, she hated herself for responding to him when he took her. There was no help for it—it was the way she was. More than once she had cursed the fate that had made her an albino Exotic.

Stark solved her dilemma by rolling from his back onto his side, facing away from her. Juete moved quickly, so that the bed's motion caused by her leaving would be unnoticed in his changing of position.

She stood next to the bed for a moment and waited for

his breathing to resume the cadence of deep sleep, then moved quietly away to the fresher. Inside, she shut the door and dialed the light up slightly, but not to full brightness. She sat on the covered bidet and drew her feet up to touch her bare buttocks, clasping her arms around her knees. She took several deep breaths, letting them out softly.

After a moment, the tears began to flow. She cried silently, mouth open wide so he would not hear her sobs. When he slept was her only time alone, the only time she could be reasonably sure that he would not send for her. If he caught her crying, he would demand to know what was wrong. When she had first arrived, she had thought to blame the tears on things around her. Once she had said a prisoner had spoken harshly to her. For that lie, the man paid with his life. Juete could not forget that, no matter how she tried. That was when she knew that she was his slave, now and forever.

He owned her. Her sentence had been commuted—he didn't know that she knew—and she was certain that he meant to take her with him when he left the Cage. That was all that kept her going—the thought that someday she might leave this hellish planet. Even as his slave, there was a chance she could escape him once they were back on a civilized world.

Stark wanted her to love him; Juete could feel that as she had felt it with a dozen others. They all wanted her, but they also wanted her to love them, body and soul and mind, exclusively and forever. She had withheld that from him, had kept it as her final trump. When he was transferred, as someday he must be, she would play it then, pretend to give him that which he wanted so much. Once he believed that she loved him, he would relax his vigilance. And once he loosened his hold on her, even a fraction, she could flee.

The tears flowed faster as she thought about escape. To

be free, to have the choice of where to go, and with whom, that was her goal. Without it she would have no reason to continue living. With it, there was hope, however small and distant it might be.

"Juete?"

The sound froze her, even sleep-fogged as it was. She wiped the tears away with both hands as though he could see through the panel.

"In the fresher," she called.

"Hurry back," he said. His voice was more awake now. "I have a surprise for you."

The Exotic had to squeeze her eyes shut quickly to keep from crying again. Quickly, she ran cold water in the basin and washed her face and hands. She dried herself and forced a fake smile into place. *The master calls, whore. Go and give him that which he desires—for now. But someday it will change.*

Someday . . .

* eight *

Commander Karnaaj sat stiffly in the chair across from Stark, as if he were afraid that the inert chunk of furniture might swallow him alive if he relaxed in the slightest. Stark found himself struck once again by the bloodless features. Karnaaj's skin was almost as pale as Juete's.

"Is he ready to talk?" Karnaaj said.

Stark glanced away from the other man's unblinking stare. "I think not. Exposure to the other convicts affected him not at all; I threatened him with mindwipe, but if he was afraid, I could not detect it. I hesitated to utilize any stronger methods, knowing your insistance on keeping him available." *Do your own damned work,* Stark thought. *If he dies, you can't blame me for it.*

"I see." The intelligence officer removed a small flatscreen unit the size of his palm from his gray uniform tunic, thumbed up a file and glanced at it. Stark sat quietly fuming as Karnaaj ignored him. Finally, Karnaaj said, "I have business in the city."

There was no need to specify which city, as there was only one of any size on Omega. "It will take perhaps a week or ten days to attend to," Karnaaj continued. "When

I return, the prisoner should be ready to tell me what I wish to know.''

Stark could not resist the temptation. ''Oh? And how is this to be accomplished, Commander?''

This time Karnaaj smiled, very slightly. ''Use the Zonn Chamber.''

Stark sat up in his chair, astonished. ''I thought you wanted information from him. The Zonn Chamber will reduce him to a gibbering wreck! No human or mue has ever come out sane after more than a day or two in it.''

''You will find that Dain Maro isn't quite as fragile as that, if our information is correct.''

''And if your information is incorrect?''

Karnaaj smiled again, stretching his thin lips slightly but still not showing any teeth. ''Then you will have the satisfaction of seeing me proved wrong, Commander Stark. A pleasure for you, I am certain it will be.''

''Whatever can you mean, Commander? Why should I take any pleasure from the distress of a fellow Confederation officer?'' Stark's voice was bland, but there was no hiding how he felt from himself. He would *love* to see Karnaaj fall flat. He would never say that, of course; his computer was recording the conversation, and he was willing to bet a thousand standards to a toenail that Karnaaj's flatscreen also had a vocalstat working.

Karnaaj made a small gesture of dismissal. ''In any event, I suggest that you incarcerate Maro in the Zonn Chamber immediately. I would also suggest that he be monitered at eight hour intervals. I leave the state of his sanity to your judgement. Remove him when you think he is willing to respond to my questions.''

''Wait just a moment, Commander—''

''You have doctors, Warden. Surely you can manage to keep one prisoner mentally healthy for a few days.''

Stark started to reply, then stopped. This was all being recorded, he reminded himself. Carefully, he said, ''On your orders, then, Commander Karnaaj, I shall incarcerate prisoner Dain Maro in the Zonn Chamber. I shall utilize my best efforts to maintain his sanity until your return; however, I cannot guarantee this. The Zonn Chamber is poorly understood by our science. I can hardly be blamed for its effect upon a man's mind."

Karnaaj grinned wider, showing perfect teeth. "Yes you can, Warden. You are aiding the *Soldatutmarkt* in its investigation into intragalactic criminal activites, but Maro is *your* prisoner. I have told you to use your judgement in utilizing my *suggestion* that you place Maro in a portion of the prison for which *you* have been given responsibility. By assuming this command, you have indicated your fitness to hold it. You have more practical experience in using the Zonn artifacts than most scientists; therefore, you are to use this practical knowledge to aid me in my investigation." He stood. "I have indicated where your responsibility lies. See that you understand this, Warden."

Oh, I understand, Stark thought. *You have put the responsibility on my shoulders well enough. If I screw up, my head will roll. My only consolation is that yours will probably roll next to mine, and I find that scant comfort.*

"I'll have a guard escort you out, Commander Karnaaj."

"No need. I know the way."

Juete was on her way to Stark's office when the thin, cadaverous man wearing the uniform of a Confederation officer appeared at the corridor's intersection in front of her. Karnaaj. She knew of him; most albinos on the Darkworld had heard of him, for Karnaaj had "owned" no less than three Exotics, at no small cost for the illegal slavery involved. She had heard the horror stories, had even known one of the families from which the Confed soldier had taken one of his victims. While nearly all humans and mues felt an attraction to Exotics, Karnaaj apparently felt it to an unusual degree. Two women and one man, hardly more than a boy, really, had been sold to him. And all three had died beneath his ministrations.

They had not, she had heard, been pleasant deaths.

Karnaaj saw her, and his smile seemed to take over his face. He stopped in front of her, and she knew it would be foolish to try to go around him.

"Ah. You would be Juete, Stark's Exotic." He let his gaze travel up and down her body slowly. Juete repressed a shudder. She had felt the touch of thousands of admiring looks, but none so chilling as this.

Karnaaj put out a hand as if to feel the firmness of her shoulder. Juete pushed the hand away. The man laughed. "Ah, a sense of self! I like that!" Abruptly his smile faded, and the look that replaced it was more akin to hunger. All humor was gone from his voice when next he spoke. "You are beautiful, of course, but more so than even other Exotics I have known. You could keep a man very happy, I have no doubt." He paused, and the smile returned, but it no longer hid the desire. "Would you like to leave Omega? I can arrange it, you know. You can be a free woman again."

Dumbly, Juete shook her head. Freedom with this man would be short and painful, and the end of it would be the final chill.

His smile vanished, replaced this time by anger. "It doesn't matter what you want, slut! It is not your choice to make. I shall have you—my only regret is that I must wait until I return before it happens."

Juete felt cold settle into her, an icy sensation that sheathed her like a splash of liquid air. Karnaaj reached out again and cupped her breast with one thin hand. She made no move to prevent it. He kneaded her breast, not gently, pinching the nipple until it stirred and erected under his thumb and forefinger. "Already your body desires me. I know you people. You may hate me with your mind, but your flesh aches for my touch. Soon, my sweet child—soon."

He stroked her face once, using one finger, then walked away.

He was right. She hated him, she hated *all* of them who used her and her kind as sexual toys, without any thought for the mind behind the desirable body. But she also could not deny her genetic code, and he was right about the desire. The flesh was weak; it had been programmed to be so, and it would always remain so.

As Karnaaj's footsteps died away, Juete turned and saw Stark standing in the doorway to his office. She was an expert on human emotion; she could read body language like a basic primer. The look on his face held fear, rage, jealousy, and lust. She had seen the latter three on him before, but the first, fear, was new.

Despite the precariousness of her situation, she enjoyed seeing Stark afraid. She started toward him, wondering how much of what Karnaaj had said she would tell her current jailer. All of it, she decided. That would make him worry even more, and he deserved all the worry she could provide him.

Scanner had duty in the library again, but he sent Chameleon to tell Maro about the Zonn. Maro was working an ancient floor buffer over the worn wood of the dining hall. The machine's robotics kept sticking in a diagonal pattern, and he had to stop every few minutes to reprogram the correct sequence.

Chameleon looked ten years younger than when Maro had seen him last. His hair was red now, and little more than a fuzzy cap. His eyes had turned green.

"Nobody knows what the Zonn looked like or where they went," Chameleon told him. "Scattered around the galaxy are ten cities like the one the Cage is built around, mostly high-walled. If they left anything else, half a million years took care of it. That's how long the scientists figure they've been gone.

"Scanner says he's checking on that stuff you told him about. Seems there are some interesting experiments going on as to the exact nature of the Zonn walls. I dunno all the technical shit he spouted, but he says we're dealing with energy more than mass, and your comment about the Bender fits right in. He also says the impossible might take a little longer."

Maro grinned. The buffer started off on a tangent again, and he went to stop it. He punched in the code once more, and after a few seconds the machine resumed its back-and-forth pattern. Beneath its brushes the floor gleamed dully.

"But there's bad news, too," the face dancer continued. "Karnaaj just left, and the word is that you are to go into the Zonn Chamber."

"What's that?"

Chameleon shivered theatrically. "Nobody knows for sure. It's the only place in the prison that is completely enclosed by Zonn material. Some rooms have incorporated one or two walls, but the Zonn Chamber has four, plus the floor. The only way in or out is through a door in the ceiling, which is man-made. People put inside go crazy after a little while. It does something to your mind."

"What?"

Chameleon shrugged. "The ones who just went in and came right out talked about nightmares and visions. The ones left in for a while don't talk about anything—anything that makes sense, that is."

"The Demon Graveyard," Maro said softly.

"What?"

"Nothing. Just something I learned once about concentration."

"Yeah, well, Scanner says to come by the library when you get off; he wants to talk to you."

"Copy that."

"And Maro—good luck. I wouldn't want to be you right now."

Stark tried to keep the smile fixed in place, but it was hard. His guts churned when he thought about Juete with Karnaaj. The man was a powerful enemy, and he did not doubt that he would try to take Juete from him. Stark did not think he had the clout to stop him in a showdown. But there were other ways.

Juete stood watching him. "You are going to have an accident," he said to her. "A fatal one. When Karnaaj gets back, he won't find you."

Her face lit with fear.

"No, no, not really," he said quickly to reassure her. "I'll hide you until he is gone. We'll fake an accident, cremate a body, and show him the ashes. After he's gone you can come out, and things will go back to normal."

She relaxed somewhat. "I'll have to keep you out of sight," Stark continued. "There are some cells in solitary . . . I'll have some nice things installed for you—"

"Alone? You'll make me stay *alone*?" The fear had returned to her face, and her voice now held a deep measure of horror.

"Just for a little while. A few weeks—"

"No! I can't! You don't understand! I can't be alone, I need to be with people!"

"It's only a temporary measure," he said, trying to calm her.

"I'll *die!*"

He felt himself beginning to lose patience. "Don't be absurd. You don't understand; I'm trying to protect you—"

"*You* don't understand! I'm an Exotic; I *have* to have people to talk to, to touch, to be with!"

His jaw muscles danced as he clamped down on his anger. He was doing this for her, was she so stupid she couldn't see that? He realized it would be hard on her, but it was the lesser evil. "There is no other choice," he said.

"There are always other choices! You could kill him!"

"Calm down, Juete—"

He put his hands on her shoulders, and at his touch she became abruptly still; the tension seemed to discharge from her, to be replaced with a lassitudinious resignation that was even more upsetting to him. "All right," she said dully. "You are my keeper; I must obey you."

That was her most painful barb, one that always sank the deepest into his heart. Not "I love you and do this because you wish it," but "I obey because you order it." He would do almost anything to avoid hearing that slavelike tone in her voice. Almost anything, but not this. Giving her up for any reason was too much. Especially to an animal like Karnaaj. He had to hide her.

"I will make it up to you after he is gone, I promise. And I'll visit you every day. You'll have a transceiver, so we can talk, and a holoproj and recordings to watch. Books and games and music, too. It won't be as if you are stranded on some barren asteroid or something."

"Anything you say," she said listlessly.

* nine *

The warden himself escorted Maro to the Zonn Chamber, along with Lepto and another guard. The latter were both armed with spetsdöds. Maro had once been hit by one of the chemical flechettes that the little dart guns molded to the back of the hand fired, and the headache that had followed his awakening had been memorable. He had no intention of trying to fight. He found it interesting, though, that the warden was concerned enough that he brought along two armed guards.

They came to a wall of Zonn material, gunmetal blue and cold. A narrow wooden stair had been built next to it, and Lepto gestured with the hand that wore the weapon that Maro should climb the steps.

At the top was a platform of ferrofoam, into which a trap door had been cut. The second guard followed Maro and swung the door open. A synlon rope ladder lay piled on the roof next to the trap door. The guard shoved the ladder into the dark opening.

"Any final words?" the warden asked.

Maro shook his head.

"Inside, then. Somebody will be back in eight hours to check on you. If you're ready to tell the SIU what they want to know, you can come out. Otherwise . . ." Stark nodded toward the opening.

Maro said nothing. He grabbed the smoothly braided top rung and descended into the chamber.

When he reached the bottom the ladder was withdrawn. The heavy door swung shut after him. The darkness was very quiet. Maro looked around. The room was fairly large, about four meters by six meters, with a ceiling three meters high. There was barely enough light to see by, though where it came from he could not have said. The ceiling was of ferrofoam, but the featureless walls and floor were all courtesy of the Zonn. In the far corner was a chemical toilet and cabinet with meager depil, soap and towels. A fan-folded bed completed the picture.

He spotted the photomutable gel eye of the holocam mounted opposite the toilet, where Scanner said it would be. He turned away from the optical and put a hand to his face, as if rubbing his jaw, using the motion to hide what he was really doing: spitting the ear-and-throat patch transceiver Scanner had given him into his hand.

"It might not work," Scanner had told him. "About half the time, the spy gear they got in there puts out nothing but wavy green lines on the holoproj. But if you cover the earpatch with your hair and stick the throat patch low, so the coverall hides it, we might be able to talk. I used a shielded circuit chip so you won't bleed into another frequency, but there's no guarantees. Don't use it unless you really need to."

"Thanks, Scanner. I owe you."

"Nothing is what you owe me. That info you gave me on the Zonn might just get us out of here. I still need some more, though. I've tapped into a Confed opchan, a straight link to the archives on Bocca. If you're right, we might have something. But there's things you know you aren't saying yet, I take it?'

Maro had nodded. "Yes. Something I paid a lot for when I found out I was coming here."

"I thought so. And we'll need it, so we need you."

"I'll try to stay in one piece."

"That's not a problem in the Zonn chamber. Trying to stay sane is. Call if it gets bad. Maybe I can help, somehow."

Now, in the chamber, he felt the pressure of whatever mental energies the Zonn had left imbued in their technological marvels. There was a strong sense of alien *others* tapping at the entrance to his mind. It came faintly at first, like gentle whispers on a stray breeze.

Being other whither which?

Proud see hold clear open open open!

He felt a quick lance of fear, which he managed to dispel. He combed his hair with his fingers, surreptitiously setting the receiving part of the compatch behind his ear as he did so. Then he scratched his neck and stuck the throat patch into place.

If he was to use it, he would have to subvocalize, so that the cell's sound gear would not hear him. Or maybe he could just rant and pretend to be talking to invisible friends. That would be a nice touch.

At the moment, however, Maro had to fight the sense of suffocation that enveloped him. He grabbed the thin towel from the rack and folded it, then sat on it in the middle of the room, feeling instinctively that it was better not to have direct contact with the coldness of the Zonn construct any more than he could help. And he most certainly did not want to fall asleep, so the bed was out.

He sat tailor-fashion on the folded towel, his hands in his lap. He needed to erect a mindshield immediately. He took several cleansing breaths, then closed his eyes and began.

When he had reached a fairly high level of meditation during the Soul Meld training, his instructors had used an enecephalocaster to create the illusion called the Demons' Graveyard, as a test of his concentration. It had been a terrifying experience, one which many of his fellow students had failed. Maro had survived, but it had not been easy.

It had been simple enough to understand the goal: to spend the night in a graveyard filled with demons who try to devour your essence. If you concentrated properly, you could defeat them; if not, they could engulf your soul and you would suffer the tortures of the worst possible hell.

It had been a test to concentrate his *ki,* his mental power. He had passed the test then, and he intended to pass it now.

But even as he built up his mindshield, using the meditative techniques he had practiced for years, he felt the demons gathering in the darkness outside his sanity. They were infinitely more powerful than those he had faced before. He could feel fear beginning to crack the foundations of his shield . . .

"He's just sitting there, Warden. Like before."

Stark switched his com off with a savage twist. It had been four hours. Usually by this time, prisoners were swearing, screaming to be set free, crying or laughing hysterically. But none of them had ever just squatted in the goddamned cell and done *nothing!*

As much as it galled him to admit it, Stark realized that Karnaaj had been right. This Maro had something going for him, something that set him apart from and above the rest of the scum under his jurisdiction. Aside from his irritation at the fact, something he couldn't quite touch gnawed at a distant corner of his mind—an uncomfortable sensation that made him want to turn around and look behind him. This could lead to trouble, and he had enough of *that* dealing with Juete and that bastard Karnaaj.

He looked at his chronometer. He'd promised Juete he

would come to see her at least twice a day, and already he was late for the first visit. Karnaaj was not due back in the Cage for some time yet, but Stark was taking no chances—he had had her incarcerated today. She had pleaded and begged again for him to reconsider—the little fool! Couldn't she see he was doing this for her own good?

Obviously not. But that wouldn't stop him.

Juete sat on the bunk in the cell, staring at the wall. What she felt was called eremophobia; that was the name the doctors gave it. It was common among certain populations, notably the albinos on Rim, also called the Darkworld, in the Beta System. Eremophobia: the fear of being alone. Among her people such a fear was inbred, as much a part of their genetic makeup as pheromonic attractiveness and white skin. The warped genius who had stirred the chromosomal stew that resulted in albino Exotics had certainly known how to get what he wanted.

She stared at the wall, ignoring all the toys Stark had installed for her comfort. The holoproj sat next to the laser ball recorder; the special com link she could use to call Stark anytime rested atop a carton of recording spheres holding a thousand hours of entertainment vids. The games computer that could transform the 3-D playing field into any one of a hundred arenas of sport had yet to be activated. The automated food and drink processor hummed to itself, waiting patiently for her first request.

Juete reached for the comset for the tenth time, then pulled her hand back. No. It had only been a few hours—she knew that, even though she had turned off the holoproj's clock. If he knew how much she wanted to talk to someone, to *anyone*, then sooner or later he would use it against her. It had been a mistake to lose control and tell him about her fears. Most norms didn't know about that. Some did—she had no doubt that Karnaaj knew—but it was not something Exotics let slip very often. That knowledge simply gave their masters another weapon to use, and they had too many already.

Control yourself, Juete. There are hundreds of people within a few dozen meters. You can't see them, but they are there, just down the hall, in cells all around you. You aren't alone, not really.

It did not help. She could feel the walls around her, solid and impassable. It was hard to breathe; she had to strain to keep the air flowing. If she didn't concentrate, she knew she would suffocate. And the terror that rode her whispered to her: What if something happened to Stark? What if he had an accident, or was attacked by an inmate? Nobody else knew she was here. If something happened to him, she would stay here forever. She would die here, alone, alone, *alone* . . .

Stop it!

She moved from the bed, itself padded with thrice the normal mattress material, and walked to the processor. He had included wine as one of the selections, a local product produced in small quantities for offworld export. It was not bad, so she punched in the code for it.

A soft plastic cup dropped into the loading slot, and a thin stream of dark red began to pour into it. When it was full, Juete removed the cup and drank the cool liquid in three large swallows. She hesitated a moment, then repeated the request code for more.

By the fourth cup, she felt somewhat better. The fear had not left, but it had lost some of its sharp focus. As she sipped at the fifth cup of wine, she came to realize that there was nothing else she could do to maintain her sanity at this point. As long as the wine held out, she would be all right. The processor had to contain at least four or five liters, didn't it? At least that.

At least that.

* * *

When he arrived at Juete's cell, Stark was amazed to find her drunk. He had never seen her that way before. She had told him that sex was the opiate of the Exotics, and that most rec-chem held little pleasure for them. There was no denying her inebriated state, however.

"Well, hello there!" she said brightly.

Stark stared at her. She was naked, gloriously so, and practically threw herself on him when he entered the cell. She began to kiss him and thrust her pelvis against him, touching him expertly with her magic hands. He could smell the wine on her breath, but he nevertheless found himself responding to her passion. She tugged his clothes from him so quickly that he later had trouble believing he could strip so fast. They fell on the floor.

He came fast, the first time, as she pounded him from above, riding with a frenzy he had never seen. It was her show; she was in command, and it was all he could do to keep up, even as excited as he was. Juete timed her motions so that her climax matched his, and she screamed when they spasmed together.

When it was done, Stark lay listening to his heart thumping, feeling the surge of his pulse all over his body. He was dazed; she had never unleashed herself like this before. It was at once exciting and somehow frightening. This was how he wanted her to be with him; he wanted her passion and her love, and this was at least half of his desire.

He stroked her back as she lay on him, her face pressed against his shoulder, her lips gently nibbling his skin. Other than her ebullient greeting she had not spoken, save for the wordless scream at her orgasm, and neither had he said anything. Her skin felt cool on his, and he slid his hands down to cup her buttocks before softly dragging his fingers up over her back.

She shuddered, and he felt a wetness on his shoulder

and chest then. After a moment, he realized that it wasn't sweat but tears. She was crying.

For the briefest of moments, he wondered if her tears might be from sadness. Then, she began to move on him again, sliding up and down with delicious friction, and he knew that the tears had to be from happiness. It was happening, as he had always hoped it would: she was learning to want and love him. It had to be.

Her eyes were closed as she sat up and rode him again. To his disbelief, he found himself able to respond, leaning back so he could reach deeper into her. Her tears still trickled down her pale and beautiful face, but now his passion ruled him again, and he thought no more about them.

ten

The demons were subtle now. At first they had thrown themselves against the power of his mindshield like insects against the windscreen of a fast aircar. They could not force themselves inside, but they could send their thoughts through, as sound passes through a solid metal wall.

Holdstrong never to be one . . .

listenlistenlisten hear not . . .

Pretends. Then lies of fear . . .

Nay, lies of truth, more fear . . .

Maro "heard" the alien thoughts, though he was not sure if they were in fact truly alien, or his own thoughts somehow twisted by the surrounding aura of the Zonn construct. For the strange walls and floor surely gave out some form of energy—he could sense it, could almost *taste* it far back in his throat. The question was an intellectual exercise for which he did not have the time to consider, however; he was too busy fighting for his mind.

And there came truth: always more painful than the most horrendous lie when used properly. He saw:

—The ten-year-old Dain Maro running with his best friend, fleeing the farmer whose sugarfruit tree they had just raided. His friend stumbled and sprawled on the soft ground of the orchard, his sack of booty spilling like giant green marbles. "Dain!" he yelled. "Help me!" But Maro kept running, afraid of the swearing man behind them, his bowels knotted in fear, wanting to help his friend, but afraid, afraid . . .

—Dain Maro at sixteen, lying to the girl he wanted to make love to, telling her he loved her when all he wanted was her body: "No, Melin, really, I *do* love you, I want to prove it to you . . ."

—Maro the student, wanting to learn the mysteries and realizing that he had neither the patience nor the stamina to slog through ten more years of training in the priesthood: "You're afraid to teach me; I'm ready, I know it, and you know it too! Show me . . ."

—Maro in a barroom fight, facing a bigger, stronger man, pounding on the man past the point of stopping the fight, but enjoying the feel of beating the miserable son-of-a-bitch . . .

—Maro locked in the Zonn chamber, his mind dribbling away, losing control, becoming little more than a mindless hulk, doomed to a life of gray, empty thoughts . . .

"No!" he shouted. And with that single denial he wrenched himself away from the demonic chatter, retreating, running down never-used corridors within his own mind, slamming massive doors behind him. And eventually he came to a place of peace within himself, a chamber lit with a white glow by a crackling globe of energy that floated at chest height in the center of the small room. From the ceiling, a lance of electrical fire fed the globe, a beam of universal energy that had many names: *ki,* life force, *kundalini, mana,* the Christ, the Buddha, and *ka,* the soul.

The construct that was Maro took a deep breath, drawing in the energy and filling himself with it. He knew this place. It was his Center, his very essence, and as long as he could stay here he was safe. He might die, but he would do so with his mind inviolate.

The voices still filtered through, but so faintly that they posed no threat. He was safe for now, but he knew he could not stay here forever. As long as he could maintain this vision, this sanctuary within himself that he had created, he could passively defend himself—but eventually he would grow tired, his concentration would wane, and he would lose the construct. So he knew he had to do something more active.

Within his mind, the visualization that Maro had of himself sat down on the cool floor of his sanctuary. He locked his legs in the lotus knot, closed his eyes and concentrated. After a moment he rose from the floor and began to float; a few centimeters at first, then he began moving upward faster. He drifted up past the glowing globe, until he was facing the bolt of constantly flowing energy that fed the globe that was his essence. He willed himself forward, and after a heartbeat, he entered the coruscating stream. It splashed over his face and shoulders, running down and into the body of his image, continuing on to the globe below. He could feel it revitalizing him: he was filled with raw power, a new-born star, a fount of cosmic force. He extended his arms to the sides and the lightning flowed out into his hands. Discharges bled from his fingers, dancing lines of white, particle streams rising from their own heat.

After a moment he sent his thoughts rocketing up to his control center, and with the speed of those thoughts he followed. In an instant, his mental image of himself was standing "behind" the thick mindshield, his body alive with the forces with which he had filled himself.

His visualization of the mindshield was that of an immensely thick wall of densecris. Outside, dimly visible through the milky barrier, the alien demons hammered against it, trying to get inside.

Maro grinned. His visualization of the room behind the mindshield—his control center—included an angled panel studded with buttons, rheostats and blinking lights. He pressed a button, and, with a sound of powerful servomotors groaning, the mindshield split in two, each side retracting slightly. For a moment, the alien presences were taken aback, and they hesitated. Then they swarmed into Maro, intent on whatever drove them.

But Maro was ready now. He raised his hands and felt the power begin to flow.

"Damn!"

Stark turned as the tech backed away from the com. The unit was smoking; electrical sparks danced across the keyboard and holoproj screen.

"What happened?"

"Damned if I know! It just blew up!"

That was impossible, but Stark did not waste time denying what he saw before him. "What about Maro?"

"He hadn't moved."

"I want somebody in there, now!'"

Juete lay sprawled on the bed, her head aching from the wine, her mouth tasting like she just mopped the floor with her tongue. She pushed herself into a sitting position, noticing the wine stains on her chest and stomach. After Stark had left, she had drunk herself into a stupor. She had begged him to stay, to take her out, she would do anything if he wouldn't leave her alone! But he had left.

She slid from the bed. She felt disgusted with herself. Her binge hadn't done any good; neither had her begging. He was gone and she was alone again.

Juete moved to the drink dispenser, nearly losing her balance, bumping into the com unit as she took the few steps needed. She punched the wine selector. More wine would take away the nasty taste in her mouth and maybe it would blunt the self-loathing she felt.

The machine whined, a sound she hadn't heard it make before, and it took a few seconds for her to realize what the mechanical drone meant: the wine container was empty.

She bent and examined the readout. Sure enough, the listing for wine showed a null next to it.

Juete hobbled back to the bed and collapsed onto it. There was nothing else alcoholic in the machine; she had checked that. Until Stark came back she had no choice but to remain sober. Damn him! Damn all of them in this filthy, stinking cage!

After a minute, she realized she had another option. She could call him; he had left her a com link. The sudden surge of hope crested like a sub-orbital shuttle, then fell back, drawn by the gravity of self-disgust she'd felt before. No. She wasn't going to beg again. She would die and rot before she called that bastard for help!

Juete lasted almost ten minutes before she reached for the com link. She hated herself, but the need for companionship—even Stark's companionship—was too great. She triggered it and drew in a breath to speak.

The aliens boiled in, gibbering, and Maro saw that they were not demons at all. They were not even real, in any physical sense. No, they were patterns of energy held within the walls, memories more than anything else. What they had been half a million years past he could not have said; what they were now were revenants, focused and kept in a kind of illusionary life by the Zonn energies that appeared to human senses as citylike constructs. He knew what they were now, and he knew what to do.

It was not that they were evil—it was just that they were so completely, totally *different* from anything a human mind could deal with that their touch brought madness. There was no reference point, no common ground on which they could commune. But, evil or not, their touch was dangerous to him—whether they knew it or not, they could destroy his mind if he let them.

There was only one way to save himself. In an instant he considered the implications and made his decision. The Zonn revenants were not truly alive—they were, as far as he could tell, patterns of memory force bound in the walls' interstices—recordings. They were not capable of generating new concepts, of being self-aware. Whether their corporeal ancestors had preserved them for the same reasons that humans preserved their dead, in hopes of somehow living again, or for some other, unfathomable reason, Maro did not know or care. It was enough to know that they were not truly alive, and that there was no other way to deal with them. The discipline he had learned from the Soul Melders allowed him to defend himself.

The image of Maro raised his hands and let the cosmic lightning flow, basting the Zonn revenants with forces they had never been designed to withstand. Their jubilation turned to terror and they would have fled, but the fire, the *Relampago,* followed them, dancing upon them as flames dance upon a stick of wood, using their substance for fuel.

It was all over in a moment. The stored memory patterns were crisped into near nothingness, and their astral ashes were reabsorbed by the Zonn fields, leaving not a trace behind.

On the floor of the cell, Maro opened his eyes. The room was empty, save for himself, and he knew he would not be bothered by the alien thoughts again. Once more he had survived the Demon Graveyard.

"Stark?" came a tiny voice from the patch over his ear.

"Who is it?" Maro subvocalized, keeping his lips still.

"Stark, it's Juete—please, I—I need to see you!" Her voice bordered on hysteria, Maro realized. Juete. The Exotic.

Was this another trick of some sort, instigated by the Zonn patterns? No. He had destroyed them, of that there was no doubt. Some subtle psychological trick by Stark, then? Perhaps—but the desperation in the woman's voice was so real that he could not help replying.

"Juete—this is Dain Maro. I saw you outside the warden's office."

A moment of silence; then, "Where is Stark? How did you get on this line?"

"I don't know. I'm in a special cell. There are some strange energies in here; maybe they've screwed up normal radio transmission."

"I need Stark! I'm *alone* in here!"

"I'm alone, too. In solitary."

There was a long pause. "Are you afraid?"

He no longer was, but he still heard the fear in her voice. "Yes. I'm afraid. Maybe we can help each other fight the fear."

"Oh, yes. Thank you. Thank you."

The ceiling door swung open, and Stark and a guard leaned into the room, staring down at Maro, who still sat in the center of the cell. "Maro!" Stark called.

Maro looked up at the warden. "I'm here."

"Are you ready to tell us what we want to know?"

"No."

"Fine. Then stay down there with the monsters!"

The door slammed shut, and Maro grinned. The warden didn't know that his chamber of horrors no longer worked. Good. Maybe the next man stuck in here would have sense enough to keep his mouth shut, too. It might go on a long time before Stark figured it out. Maro hoped so.

"Juete?"

"Here."

"Tell me about yourself. I need to hear your voice."

* * *

In her cell, Juete took a deep breath and allowed it to escape slowly. She could feel Maro almost as if he were here in the room with her; a warm presence on the other end of the link, somebody who cared about her. Somebody who was isolated and trapped, as she was. She felt a sense of solidarity, of common purpose. Maro hadn't put her here. Maro was a pawn, just as she was, and so she could talk to him as she had not talked to anyone since she had left the Darkworld, so many years before.

"I had two brothers," she said. "Both died before they were twenty, killed in fights. My mother was murdered, and I never knew my father. And now I'm here, for killing the son of a powerful man. He used me, and when I could, I killed him. I used a pruning laser on him, cut him in half. I would do it again."

"It's all right," Maro said. "I understand.

"Do you? Do you really?"

"Yes."

And she believed him, that was the surprise of it for her. There was something in the tone of his words, something in his voice that convinced her. Some kind of . . . calmness permeated his speech. He had nothing to gain from her, he couldn't touch her, and yet he was willing to talk to her. And so she believed him. And she could help him as well; he was alone, just as she was. That was important, to be needed, as well as wanted. Nobody had ever needed her before, not since her family had died. Everybody had wanted her, many had had her, but nobody *needed* her.

That was important. It warmed her in a way no man's or woman's touch had ever warmed her. She had never loved a man, and she knew she didn't love this Dain Maro—not yet, at least—but there was a potential here she had never felt before.

"Tell me about you," she said. "Please."

* eleven *

Maro lay on the bed, staring at the ceiling. It was the only place in the cell he could look at for long periods of time without discomfort—staring at the featureless pellucid surfaces of the Zonn walls and floor made him feel as if he were falling into them.

"Dain?"

The voice belonged to Scanner, and it came from the compatch receiver stuck behind his ear. He subvocalized his reply. "Yeah."

"Listen, we're collecting the stuff you wanted. Some of it won't be easy, though. We got Parker, the fat guard on shop detail, helping us."

"How?"

He could hear the chuckle in Scanner's voice as the circuit-rider answered. "He thinks he's giving me parts to build a 3-D pornoproj." Maro chuckled as well.

"So, how are you holding up?"

"Fine. I think their camera is broken; somebody keeps coming in to check on me every hour or so."

"What about the hallucinations? They're supposed to be pretty bad."

"I think whatever caused that is broken, too. It's no worse than ordinary solitary."

Silence for a moment. "You did something." It was not a question.

Maro thought about it for a couple of seconds before he answered. It wouldn't hurt at this point if the prisoners thought he held some kind of ace. He needed their help, and they would help more if they really believed that he could pull this whole plan off. "Yeah. I took care of it. Nobody will ever have problems in here again."

"Amazing. How?"

"Trade secret. Never mind. Do you understand what I want you to do with the gear?"

"I understand the theory. I don't know if I can hardwire the system."

"You can. Did you ask your link for the plans for a single-passenger Bender unit?"

"I got them."

"Good. See if you can get a phase generator circuit chip, and a Peen stasis unit."

"I see what you're getting at, but I checked on something last time I was online. It's been tried, Maro. It doesn't work."

"Not on regular walls, you're right. But we're dealing with something that only *looks* like a wall here, Scanner. It's an energy field, and I think it will Bend."

"I hope you know what you're talking about."

Maro stared at the ceiling. The trapdoor opened and a guard stuck his head inside. Maro closed his eyes against the bright light. *I hope I do, too,* he thought.

Stark's nervousness translated into movement. He tapped his fingers on his desk, shifted in his chair, and finally stood and paced around the office. When he couldn't stand it any more, he went outside into the heat, his cooler humming into life and rolling after him.

Why wasn't Maro climbing the walls in the Zonn Chamber? Nobody had ever come out of there unchanged, and most had gone totally insane by this time. Yet, as far as he could tell, Maro was unaffected. That didn't fit into his plans at all. Karnaaj would be coming back any time now, and when he did, Stark did not want him around for very long. The SIU man would not like the story that Juete had died. Probably he wouldn't believe it, but there would be no way to disprove it, and once he had accomplished his business with Maro, there would be no further reason for him to stay around. He did not know the prison well enough to find Juete, and once he was gone, life would go back to normal.

A guard waved at him as he passed, and the warden nodded mechanically. He was not due to visit the albino girl for several more hours, and, while he would have spent more time with her, he did not want to be caught there if Karnaaj showed up unexpectedly early. It would be exactly like the bastard to do that. Juete did not like being alone, that was apparent enough, but she would just have to make do. Sometimes she seemed to forget that she only survived here because of his intervention. She had a treasure hoard of supplies in that cell with her; she should be grateful instead of whining about being alone.

He stopped walking, finding himself in a half-windowed corridor overlooking the prison infirmary. Prisoners moved around in the atrium below, and he saw a man wrapped in bandages lying in a bed. Somebody caught by a flock of bloodbirds, he remembered.

No, it wasn't fair to blame Juete for his irritation. It was Karnaaj and that goddamned Maro who deserved the anger. Karnaaj for what he was, and Maro for not rolling over and saving him all this trouble.

Abruptly, Stark turned away from the infirmary. The Zonn Chamber was not going to be the answer for Maro—he knew that now. Maybe he could find out more by releasing him back into the general population and prodding him with one of his dips. If Maro let something slip to one of the dozens of spies working for Stark, the warden would know it before the echoes stopped. That might be a way to do it. He hoped he still had time; Karnaaj was not due back for five or six days yet. A few days might be enough. If worse came to worst, there was always a way out: the mindwipe might dredge up enough to satisfy Karnaaj. Maro would not be Maro afterward, but that was too bad. It would be his own fault.

Being alone was not quite so bad, now that she had a link with Dain. The cell did not seem as confining, now that she knew she could talk to him whenever she wished. At first, she had worried that Stark might overhear, but Dain had reassured her that the channel was private. He had a friend who had taken care of that.

"Juete?"

"Right here."

"It looks as if Stark is going to let me out. The Zonn Chamber didn't produce the results he wanted."

She felt a sudden needle of fear, but before she could speak, he wiped the pain away. "I'll keep this circuit open."

"What will you do?" she asked. "Karnaaj is coming back."

"I have a couple of ideas." There was a long silence. Then, "How much do you want to get out of here, Juete?"

"That's a silly question. How much do *you* want to leave?"

He didn't answer that, but said instead, "Is there a Zonn wall in your cell?"

"Yes, the back one. Why?"

Another silence came, and she felt as if he were making some kind of decision. Finally, he spoke. "Listen, I think there's a way out. It's a long shot, and even if it works, it'll be dangerous. Some of us are going to try to escape. I think it can be done. I'm betting my life on it. If the plan goes like I hope, there's no reason why you can't come along. If you want to."

She felt her heart beating faster. "No one has ever escaped before," she said.

"I know. But there's always a first time for everything."

Juete thought about the life she had in the Cage. Of spending years inside, with Stark as her master and keeper. And that was the best scenario she could imagine. There were men like Karnaaj, there would always be people like him, waiting to prey on those without the power to protect themselves. She was alive here, but the quality of her life left no room for growth, for pleasure, for joy. What did she have to lose?

"Yes," she said. "I want to go."

"Good. I'll keep in touch. It won't be long. It'll either work or it won't—we'll know pretty soon."

She heard the electronic locking mechanism whine on the cell door. "It's Stark," she whispered. "I have to go."

"Call me when he's gone," he said.

When Stark entered the cell, Juete wore a smile for him. He hugged her, and she returned the embrace, but the desperate quality was gone. She had to give him credit for some preception; he noticed the lack.

"What's wrong?"

"Nothing. I'm fine. Glad to see you."

He untabbed the front of his coverall, grinning. "I'm glad to see you, too."

Afterwards, he lay with her on the bed.

"So, how are things out there?"

"Not much different. That bastard Maro didn't crack in the Zonn Chamber. Some kind of mind control, I think. Karnaaj knew. The rinthsucker is setting me up to fall if he doesn't get what he wants from Maro."

"What can you do about it?"

"Not a lot. He said he'd be in the city for a week, but he could come back at any time. And if I don't have Maro ready to leak information like an unshielded microwave caster, Karnaaj will skewer me, somehow."

"Can't you convince this Maro to give you what Karnaaj wants?"

"I don't think so." He shifted on the bed and cupped one of her pale breasts. Inwardly, she shuddered; no ripple of it showed on the pale surface.

"Then you're in danger?" she said.

"Maybe not." He rubbed the pink nipple with his thumb and forefinger. It erected under his touch. "I have a final token I can play in this little game. I can mindwipe Maro, if it comes to that. I'm hoping he'll spill something to one of my dips with the right prodding, but if he doesn't, I can clean his slate and give the recording to Karnaaj in a neat little package."

He leaned over then and kissed her on the neck, and she stroked his back mechanically as she thought about what he had said. A week. Dain only had a week at most, to make good his—and their—escape. After that he might be little more than a mental infant if Stark carried out his plan. She would have to get this information to him as soon as possible.

It was that thought which made her realize that she had shifted her allegiance from Stark to Dain Maro. Stark was her jailer and Maro might be her saviour. The choice was simple, and it had been made.

"You look pretty good for a man who spent four days in the Zonn Chamber," Sandoz said.

Maro grinned. Standing around him in the yard along with Sandoz were Scanner, Raze, Chameleon and Patch. Maro said, "Ah, I needed the rest. Nice and quiet in there.

If the warden offers it, you might spend a couple of days; it'd do you good."

"No, thanks," Chameleon said. Everybody laughed.

"So, Scanner tells us you've got a plan working. You want to let us in on it?" That from Raze.

Maro nodded. "I need a couple of minutes with Scanner, first. You can listen."

The circuit-rider said, "I've got the confounder specs and the basic hardwiring is done. It'll take some programming to make it work, but I think I can manage it. The biochips for the Bender and the stick-links are on the way. Parker is helping; he thinks he gets the pornoproj unit when we're done. I had to use Fish and Berque, they had contacts we needed, and I'm stalling them, but they'll want to know what we're doing pretty soon."

"Berque is a pipe to the warden, you said?"

Scanner nodded.

"All right. We can use that to feed him what we want him to know, maybe. What about Fish?"

"He's crazier than a burnt din, but he wants out pretty bad. I dunno. You'll have to decide on him."

Sandoz said, "Come on, Maro. What's the play here? Scanner has been laying smoke since you went into the Zonn Chamber."

Maro took a deep breath. "Okay. There's a theory about the Zonn: the walls of the cities they built aren't walls at all, but energy fields. And they have locked up, somehow, the same kind of power that a Bender uses to shift from real to sub-space for FTL travel. I knew some scientists who owed me favors, and I had it all checked out before they shipped me to the Cage. The story's in pieces—some on one world, some on another, some in the Galax InfoNet, some of it not. But if you put it all together, it might mean a way out."

Raze looked at Sandoz. "I think I understand. You said it before, remember?"

Sandoz looked blank.

"Through the walls," the bodybuilder said, with a short laugh. "He thinks we can walk through the walls."

Sandoz stared at Maro. "Is that right?"

Maro took a deep breath. "Yes."

"You're crazy," Sandoz said flatly.

"Maybe not," Scanner said. "We won't be able to test it until we put it all together, but it looks like it might work. Either that, or it'll clean the Cage completely off the face of the planet, along with most of the continent. We're talking a *lot* of pent energy here."

Sandoz laughed. "I like that. Go out with a bang and fuck 'em."

"That's not what we want to do," Maro said.

"Either way is fine with me," the assassin replied. "Stark loses with both. I'm in. Whatever you need me to do, let me know."

Maro nodded. "Good. Anybody else want to walk now?"

Nobody said anything.

"Good. From what I hear, we've got less than a week. Let's move."

* twelve *

When Stark left his office, it took only a second for him to notice what was missing: his cooler was not following to protect him from the heat with focused currents of chilled air. Dammit, where was it? Juete was in solitary, and it was only programmed to respond to the two of them. The heat in the hallway was not nearly as intense as it was outside, but it was enough to trigger his sweatpoint in a hurry, and the robotic sensor was tuned to that.

It took him a few minutes to find the mobile unit. It was on its back, just past the turn for the infirmary view. By this time sweat had soaked the cloth under his arms and across his shoulders and he was in no mood for jokes. One of the goddamned guards or prisoners had turtled the machine. Very funny.

As he got closer, however, he saw that the problem with the cooler was much more than a prank. The belly plate was open, and proteinprint circuit boards lay scattered and dripping around the cooler.

It had been gutted. Destroyed.

Lepto stood impassively as Stark shouted orders at him. "First, find out who had passes to be in the hall! And I want the duty roster checked! Second, figure out what biochips were taken, if any. I don't want somebody cranking up a laser on me with parts spagen-rigged from my own damned cooler! And I want all this done stat!''

''Yes sir.''

''Go! What are you standing around for?''

Lepto left, and Stark stared through the denscris window at the yard. Damn them all! The one piece of comfort he allowed himself and the bastards had killed it! Somebody was going to pay. Somebody was going to be sorry they were ever born.

''He was very upset,'' Juete said into her com.

In the shadow of the Cage's outer wall, Maro allowed himself to chuckle. ''Too bad.''

''He won't let it just lie, Dain. When he left here, he was still smoking with it. He was . . . rough with me.''

Maro felt a surge of anger curl his hands into fists. ''I'm sorry, Juete.''

''Don't be. I can deal with him. But he's got *everybody* searching for whoever wrecked his cooler.''

''He can look until he goes blind,'' Maro said. ''The pass was electronically issued and then deleted. The door computer won't remember admitting the one who did it. We're covered.''

''*Why* did you do it? It'll only make things tougher.''

''We needed a part. That was the only available place to get it.''

Silence for a moment. ''Is it going to work, Dain?''

''I think so. I hope so.''

Maro shuffled across the heat-shriveled grass toward the shade of the tool shed. As he approached he heard what sounded like a flute, and somebody singing. The voice was high and clear—a soprano—and the flute's tone almost seemed to sparkle. He listened to the words:

His face is like rainy skies, stormy and gray
She told him something bad, what he won't say
But I know if I wait awhile, the sun will shine again
On the face of my darling, my lover, my friend.

He moved closer and saw that the instrument was not just a flute, but an arofloj, an electronic version of that instrument. He didn't know who was playing it, but whoever it was was good, had programmed a whole run of contrapuntal beats to work against the melody. The singer swung into the chorus:

And I laugh when he thinks it's not funny
And sometimes I make him so mad
But he's still with me after all these years.
The best friend that ever I had.

It was Raze. To hear that sweet song coming from her muscular form astonished him. He stood silently along with a dozen others, listening until she finished the ballad. There came a strong burst of applause then, and Raze grinned at the small crowd. Most of the listeners drifted away, and Maro moved closer to Raze.

"Nice song," he said.

"Thanks. I used to sing it to my lover, back when I was in the Real Galaxy. He was a teacher; taught children how to play music. Never knew what he saw in me."

"You loved him a lot?"

"What's it to you?"

"Nothing. I liked the song."

She softened. "Yeah. He was all right, Celine was. We got along pretty good. I wonder where he is now."

"Maybe you can find out."

She turned to face him. Muscles roiled in her neck and

shoulders like a ripple spreading in a pond. "You really think we can make it out of here?"

"What have to got to lose?"

"I copy that, Slick. I'm at the point where I want to swing on Lepto every time I see him. I might even take him, but it'll cost me. Everything in here costs. Too much."

"Tomorrow night we should have everything patched together enough for a test. We'll know then if we're just spinning dust or if we have a real chance."

Raze looked at him with a peculiar expression of mingled humor and bitterness. "I don't know if I like you, Maro. You've made me hope this'll work. If it doesn't work, I'll probably be real disappointed."

He laughed. "If it doesn't work, I'll probably be real dead. And if not, you'll have to stand in line to take it out on me."

"I'll be right behind Sandoz," she said, grinning.

He returned the smile and turned to leave. "Where you headed?" she asked.

"I need to go start a pipeline to the warden. We don't want him spoiling things before we're ready."

Berque disgusted him even more, possibly, than did the Mindfucker, but Stark wore a smile for the fat man. For whatever reasons, Berque had contacts both in and outside of the Cage. And he was one of Stark's best dips. Besides, what Berque had just told him was worth a hundred smiles.

"You're sure about this?"

Berque flashed one of his own toothy grins. "Yes, Warden. We got to talking, you know how it is, about things that went down. So I asked him, 'What's all the static about you and the Confed ghoul?' He didn't want to say, at first, but I told him some stuff about me, and after a while, he opened up."

"You don't think he was just bragging?"

"Negative. I can tell when somebody is pumping sewage, believe me. I've given you some first disk material, haven't I?"

"Yes. You've been very helpful to me."

"Anyway, so after awhile, he says, 'Yeah, all he wants is to know the Black Sun dogs and whips and how the scramble runs. I can't believe they don't know about Tweel and his curs, and the bankers from Muto Kato.' "

Tweel. Muto Kato. Somebody's name, and a world in the Bruno System. He had it! "He say anything else?"

"Not anything you're interested in."

"I'm interested in *everything* he says. Listen, Berque, I want you to stay with this. Get everything you can from him. You do this right and your perks will triple."

Berque leaned back in his chair, his exopthalmic eyes almost exploding from his face. "Ah, Warden, you're too kind. Have you thought about what I asked you last time we talked?"

Stark felt his teeth grind together. He forced the smile back to his lips. "Yes, I have given it some thought. And if you get this for me, Berque, I'll see that you get the job of morgue attendant."

The fat man's smile was radiant. It made Stark's stomach turn. What Berque wanted to do with the bodies . . . well, it didn't matter. If some parts of them didn't get cremated, who would care?

When the dip left, Stark punched the names into his computer and instructed the unit to begin a search over the InfoNet. If the names looked as though they might be legitimate, he would be sitting in the pilot's seat when Karnaaj returned. Stark would make very damned sure that the Confed knew that *he* had gotten the information and not that zombie Karnaaj. He smiled at the thought. *Try to steal my woman, eh? We'll see about that, Commander Karnaaj.*

* * *

"What about your parents?" Juete asked.

In his cell, Maro smiled into the darkness. "What about them?"

"Were you happy at home? Brothers, sisters? Extended family or nuclear? Traditional or open marriage? Did you feel loved and wanted? Were your—?"

"Wait, hold it. One question at a time!"

"I'm sorry. It's only that I want to get to know all about you."

"Why? It's not that important who I was."

"Yes it is. Who you are comes from who you were. You can't escape your past; it follows you like a shadow."

He listened to the soft tones from the compatch, and smiled again. There was a lot more to this woman than met the eye. You looked at her and all you saw was the body and flawless skin, the shock of white hair and the pale eyes. And when her pheromones reached you, your own hormones stirred in response. But there was more there. She had a mind, and Maro found that more intriguing than her looks or even her enhanced sexual appeal.

"I suppose you're right. Okay. Let's go back to the first question, then. My parents. . . ."

In the quiet of his cell, separated by thick walls and distance, he told the lonely woman about himself. And found that, much to his surprise, it did not hurt at all.

When the com clicked off, Juete rolled over onto her back and grinned foolishly. It was probably too soon to tell, but she thought she loved this man. He talked to her like she was a person and not just a sexual toy. That meant more to her than she would have believed. If they were together, it would be physical—she knew that. But it would also be more. She felt a connection with Dain that she had never felt with anyone before. She liked the feeling.

Maybe his plan to escape would work. Maybe it would

not. At this point, it did not matter so much. If they could be together, even briefly, that would be worth it. She was being romantic, she knew, but she could not help the giddy feeling she had. Had anyone ever made this kind of connection long distance before? Surely someone must have. There had to be people who lived worlds apart, who talked only over White Radio or by recordings, who had come to appreciate and even love one another. Even so, it felt no less magical to her. He did not have to come for her when he escaped. But he wanted to, and that made all the difference. Dain would not use her; he would love her and respect her, she was sure of that.

Feeling that sense of newfound power, Juete no longer was afraid. She might be locked away in solitary, but she knew that she was no longer alone. She clutched that thought to herself as she fell into a peaceful sleep.

In the yard the next day, Scanner pulled Maro aside. "It's done," he said. "I don't know how long it will run, or even *if* it'll run, but it's as good as it's gonna get with what we've got."

"Can you get it to my cell?"

"Your cell? Why?"

"For the test."

"Hey, I built this twinky; *I* test it."

"It's liable to kill you, Scanner."

"Oh, and it won't kill you? What makes you immune?"

"Remember the Zonn Chamber?"

Scanner looked exasperated. "I was afraid you might say that. You think you'll need whatever you did in there to make this work?"

"I don't know. But it's better to have it and not need it—"

"—than to need it and not have it. I've heard the argument before."

Maro grinned and slapped him on the shoulder. "If it works, you'll be the first to know."

"And if not, you will."

Maro shrugged. "It's a risk. Somebody's got to take it, and it was my idea."

The thin man made a gesture of capitulation. "Okay. I'll get it into your cell. But Maro—if you blow us all up I am really going to be pissed at you."

"Just tell me what I need to know to work it."

"Right. The confounder first. There are two circuits, and an automatic synch mode that trips back and forth . . ."

Maro listened carefully as Scanner explained the workings of the Bend unit. He felt a fluttery sensation, as if something was confined in his belly and was unhappy about it. After lights out tonight, he was going to do something no man had ever done before, and if it didn't work, he would never see another sunrise.

It was a very sobering thought.

* thirteen *

"There's something else going on," Stark said to Berque. The fat convict stood in front of the warden's desk, looking very uncomfortable.

"Something else?"

"Yes. I don't know what it is, exactly, but my sources say there's some kind of tension in the air."

Outside, as if to punctuate the comment, lightning struck one of the main wall arresters with a canvas rip and boom! The afternoon storm continued to pour rain down upon the Cage.

"I haven't heart anything unusual," Berque said.

"Have you gotten anything else from Maro?"

"No, but he's on a different shift, so I don't see him as much."

Stark drummed his fingers. "Okay, starting now you're on the same shift. And I'll see that you get a hall pass. Stick close to Maro; I want to know everything he does."

"Copy, Warden."

Juete sat on the edge of her bunk, listening to Maro's voice over the comset, her belly tight with fear.

"Tonight," he said. "If we've put it together right, there'll be no problem."

"And if you've made a mistake?"

He hesitated just a moment. "I'll call you afterward."

"Dain—"

"What?"

"I'm afraid for you."

"It's okay, hon. Really. Once we know the Bender unit works, then all we have to do is set up the rest of it."

"Dain, I—I . . ."

"Listen, it'll be okay, Juete—"

"I love you," she said softly.

There was a long silence. Then, "Yeah. I think maybe I love you, too."

The storm was in full strength now, and the tropical fury of it vented against the Cage with wind, rain and occasional flashes of lightning. A bolt hit one of the big softwood trees a hundred meters from the wall, and the superheated sap boiled almost instantaneously, causing the wood to explode.

Under the overhang of the tool shed, Maro and Scanner were effectively hidden by a waterfall of runoff.

"You sure you've got it?" Scanner asked.

"Positive."

"I'm worried about the power supply. This thing is going to draw a lot of voltage from the broadcast unit. I've rigged a series of high-storage capacitors to give you the jolt you'll need, but it's still going to show up on somebody's board when you power up. I don't think they'll have time to trace it, but—"

"Don't worry about it. It'll be late. Probably nobody will even notice it."

"Let's hope."

"Listen, Scanner, you've done a hell of a job. It'll work."

"Like I said—let's hope."

"Okay. I'm going to check on Raze and Chameleon, to see how they're doing on the other part of this."

"Watch out for Berque. He's been keeping you in sight all day, in case you haven't noticed."

"I noticed. He's in the doorway of *B* block right now."

"I won't see you again before tonight. Good luck, Maro."

"Thanks, Scanner."

It was nearly midnight. Maro sat up, slowly and quietly, on his bunk. He listened, but heard no movement in the hall. Directly across from his cell, Berque seemed to be sleeping.

Time to do it.

The equipment had been put into his mattress; it formed a hard lump under his feet. The interior of the cell was lit only from the corridor light, but that was more visibility than he wanted. The diodes on the equipment provided enough illumination to do what he needed.

He fished the two pieces of electronic wizardry from his mattress. The smaller fit comfortably within his palm, a flat plastic rectangle with a single button control. That was the confounder, and according to Scanner, it did not need to be particularly good. The telemetry for the cells was, the circuit-rider had said, very basic. Strictly biochemical-electric, no EEG, MEG or ECG monitoring. What the simadam running the scope saw was nothing more than a basic life force pattern, and the tuning was very broad. As long as anybody was inside the cell, the scope would register the minimum. It was also open-ended on the top side, so there could be five people stuffed into the small room and the machine wouldn't know.

Maro thumbed the toggle button; a red LED lit on the confounder, and he shoved the device under his blanket.

He could leave now, and cell telemetry would show him still there.

The second machine was also rectangular, but almost as large as a shoebox. The hard plastic was breached in places by biochip boards wired in at odd angles. On one end was a small cone, stolen from the dental X-ray machine in the infirmary; on the top, near the other end, were three knobs, three buttons, and a small screen for LED reads. The knobs controlled power balances; the red button powered up the unit; the yellow button built sufficient charge for it to work; the green button put the whole thing into operation. Simple.

There was a third part, but it was too large to smuggle into a cell. Scanner had installed it as part of an osmotic filtering unit in the machine shop. That was the Bender unit, essentially a device to shift a small ship into hyperspace. It was linked to this box by microwave and VLF radio transceivers, and both were connected to a mainframe computer halfway around the planet. If ever a gadget was more jury-rigged, Maro did not want to see it. And he was about to risk his life, and maybe the lives of everybody on Omega, on it.

Quickly, before he could lose his resolve, Maro took a deep breath, glanced across the hall at the supine form of Berque on his bed, then turned back toward the Zonn wall at the back of his cell. He stood carefully, facing the wall.

He was, he knew, afraid. There had been many times in his life when he had faced serious injury or death, but in almost all of those cases, he had been in control. This time he was going to have to depend almost totally on the brains and skills of others. He could stop here. He could tell them that it didn't work, and nobody would ever know. He could pull a chip or twist a wire loose. They were dealing with very potent energies, and a mistake might be violently fatal. An unchambered Bender might vibrate itself into another dimension, leaving a smoking crater a klick across behind it. Or it might do far worse than that.

For a brief moment, he felt paralyzed by the latter possibility. Did he have the right to take such a risk? There was a small but finite chance that the unit, instead of doing what they designed it for, might instead release all the bound energy of the Zonn material in a nuclear explosion that would decimate the planet. Who was he to put however many innocent people who lived on Omega in such jeopardy? The majority of them he did not know or care about, but there were his friends—and Juete. How could he risk her life—especially in light of what she was coming to mean to him?

Maro closed his eyes and shook his head savagely. They would be better off dead than doomed to a life in the Cage. And if it happened, they would certainly not suffer, just as he certainly would not be around to regret it. He let out the breath he was holding and took another.

He pushed the red button. The small flatscreen glowed into blue life, and a series of numbers lit in one corner. Power on. So far, so good.

Maro pushed the yellow button. The screen jumbled and began to scroll a series of numbers and words too fast to read. Then the crawl slowed. A bar chart appeared on half the screen, showing power to be at 90 percent maximum. Better than they'd hoped. Sweat beaded on his face; he wiped at it with the sleeve of his coverall. He pointed the cone at the Zonn wall. *Okay, Maro. This is it. Time to shoot it or rack it.*

He pressed the green button.

There came a high-pitched hum that quickly shaded off into ultrasonics. The box vibrated in his hands, and he quickly dialed down the knob on the left. Scanner had said it might do that—*Jesu Christo Jones!*

The wall ahead of him swirled. Like smoke in a slice laser, the gunmetal Zonn material *moved*. Maro watched as the hardest substance man had ever come across wiggled like current eddies on the surface of agitated water. Something was happening, that was for damned sure, but—what?

There was only one way to find out.

Maro stepped toward the wall. He half expected to have his nose smashed flat when he hit the metal—but instead he stepped *into* the wall itself.

And into another world.

Stark lay in his bed alone, wishing for the comfort of Juete next to him. Soon all this shit would be over, and he could have the albino woman back with him. Meanwhile, he would take care of business—and continue to sleep uncomfortably alone.

The com chirped on the bedside table. Who would be calling him at this hour?

"Stark here."

"Tech First Ostental, Warden. I hate to bother you, but standing orders say to call you if anything unusual happens."

Stark sighed. "Go ahead."

"We just got a call from the Bogi Desert power station. They had a surge right about 2400. Something drew nearly nine hundred thousand watts from the main generator grid all at once. Almost burned out a substation between here and there."

"So? How does that concern us?"

"They think it came from around here."

"Do we show any equipment running that would do that?"

"No, sir."

Stark sighed again. Did he have to hear about every dead fly that hit the ground? "Are there any thunderstorms on your radar, tech?"

"Yes, sir. About eighty klicks southwest of here."

"There's your answer. Probably lightning hit something

and screwed up a reading. Tell Bogi station we didn't take their juice."

"I copy that."

"And don't bother me unless something concerning prison security comes up, understand?"

"Yessir!"

"Discom." Stark dropped the comset back on the table and rolled over onto his back. He hated this place. If he didn't get out of here soon, he was going to be talking to the goddamn walls.

By all human standards, the Zonn would have to have been insane. Maro found himself not on the other side of the Zonn wall, as he had expected, but in a world of madness. There was a wall behind him, to be sure, but it reached up out of sight. Ahead of him lay a landscape of twisted columns, moving hills, and glowing blue lights that surged and faded, bright and then dimmer, all overlaid with a swirling gunmetal blue fog. He shifted his feet, and sparks danced under his boots.

He had not expected this. The walls were stable energy fields, that much he had surmised, holding the astral patterns of their ancient builders. He had expected to have to deal with them, as he had done in the Zonn chamber. But this . . . what—and *where* was it?

His first reaction was to turn and retreat back into his cell. He held that feeling in check. No, this was supposed to be a test, and only the first part of it had worked.

Scanner's cell was exactly sixty-nine steps to the right of his own. He had paced it twice, to be sure. He need only take the proper number of steps in that direction and he would be behind Scanner's cubicle. He should be able to walk through the Zonn wall in the back of the other cell just as easily as he had his own.

Might as well get moving, he thought.

He heard a voice cry out then, a ghostly yell, and he

nearly dropped the dematerializing device. He caught it quickly. Wouldn't do to break that—it was his only way out of this nightmare. The voice came again, but fainter, and he felt a sense of relief. He had fought the Zonn demons before and won, but he wasn't sure he could do so again under these circumstances. He did not want to try.

Moving with great care, Maro walked. He counted the steps aloud, his voice sounding hollow and far away.

". . . Sixty-seven, sixty-eight, sixty-nine."

He stopped. This ought to be it. Scanner had said he would keep clear of the back wall. Maro pointed the device at the infinite cliff before him. The solid-looking wall swirled as it had before, and it was with a feeling of immense relief that Maro stepped through.

And found himself in the hot night air, next to the main wall, *outside* the Cage.

Maro fought a sense of panic. This was impossible! The main wall was several hundred meters from his cell at the closest, and in another direction entirely!

After a moment, he calmed himself. *Okay, so the walls have some kind of higher dimensional aspect to them. Fine. We can deal with that. Might even make things easier. We'll all get to my cell, take sixty-nine steps, and end up outside.* He grinned. This odd Zonn construct was going to be just what they needed! The test was a success; he could tell Scanner in the morning. Right now, however, he needed to get back to his own cell.

He stepped back into the Zonn dimension. A swirl of fog blotted the blue lights for a moment, but he turned and paced off the proper number of steps back to his own cell. Still grinning, he stepped through the wall.

The grin died as he sucked in a quick breath. He was in the duty room! Just ahead of him sat the night guard, his back to Maro, watching an entertainment vid on his holoproj. The guard must have heard something, because he started to turn. Quickly, Maro spun and leaped back into the wall.

His heart pounded, and his breath came in quick, short inhalations. What had happened? He had counted the steps correctly, he was sure of it! But he was at least fifty meters off!

Maro looked at the shifting landscape, the swirling fog, and suddenly knew: the usual rules didn't apply here. Somehow, this side of the wall had changed in relationship to the other side.

How was he going to find his way back to his own cell?

The screen started to blink on the DM unit. He looked down at it. Uh-oh . . . the power reserves were down to 47 percent. How many more crossings could he make?

Could he draw more power in here? He tried, stabbing at the yellow button, but the level remained unchanged. So much for that idea.

He considered options. He would cross back into the prison, hide the DM, and hope for the best. They'd want to know how he got out of his locked cell, however, and that might put a big crimp in the escape plan. No, there must be a better way, but he couldn't keep blundering around much longer looking for it. Passing through the wall five times had used almost half his power; that meant he might have five more shots before winding up stranded. If only there was a way to get into his cell from the other side . . .

Wait. He had an idea. It depended on whether or not the wall had shifted to another place behind him. If it had, it wouldn't work. But if that guard was still there, there was a chance.

The guard was still there, still watching the holoproj. Thank the gods for that! Maro put the device down quietly, and walked up behind him. There was a pressure point on the neck, and a nerve junction . . . he chopped down hard with his right hand, at the same time stabbing with the open fingers of his left. The guard slumped over onto his control unit, unconscious. He would wake up sore and with a headache, but there wouldn't be any way he could know who had done it.

Maro studied the controls for the cell doors, set the timer, and unlocked the block admit and his own cell. He picked up the device and hurried down the dim corridor. If anybody saw him, they didn't say anything. He opened his door and moved inside, closing it behind him. Ten seconds later he heard the electronics *snick!* as his door relocked. He had made it! He felt a surge of triumph. The test had worked—partially, anyway—and he had overcome the glitches and made it back.

But his joy faded fast when he looked across the corridor and saw Berque smiling at him.

"I saw what you did," Berque said. "Take me with you when you go."

✳ fourteen ✳

Stark glared at the holoproj floating over his com unit. "I'll be there tomorrow," Karnaaj said. "I trust you will have some results for me?"

Stark made his grin as wolfish as he could. "In fact, yes. I'm checking on the information even as we speak. I have a source who has learned several things from Maro that might interest you."

"Really?" Karnaaj seemed surprised, a fact that absolutely delighted Stark.

"Yes. We have our methods also, Commander."

"I hope so, Warden. Tomorrow at 0900, then."

Stark leaned back from the com, feeling less confident. True, the InfoNet had told him that the name Maro gave to Berque did in fact exist. There were several dozen Tweels being checked, some of whom had criminal activity tied to them. Deeper investigation would no doubt reveal the proper man—or woman, if that was the case. The material on the bankers from Muto Kato was less satisfactory, it being such a broad subject to investigate, but it was progressing as well as could be expected at this point.

Now that he thought about it, something in Karnaaj's astonishment bothered Stark. It was as if the SIU man did not expect to actually learn what he purportedly wanted to know from the smuggler-turned-killer. Stark frowned. Something rang atonally here.

It wasn't just Karnaaj's reaction. Other things, little things, had been happening that bothered him. The destruction of his cooler, for example; several circuits had been stolen, although, according to his computer, it would take a genius to figure out a way to use them to make any kind of killing weaponry. And one of his guards had claimed he had been attacked last night, though there was no way it could have happened. No prisoners were missing from their cells, and all guards were accounted for according to the work plates. Stark suspected that the man had simply fallen asleep and had tried a poor excuse to cover it. There was a bruise on the man's neck, but that easily could have been self-inflicted.

It made him uneasy, though, that such odd things were happening. Maybe it was time for a full-scale security sweep, time to see what had been accumulating in the cells. There was always something—drugs, weapons, something—and it had been a while since he had shaken the place hard to see what would fall out. Yes. Before Karnaaj got here in the morning, he would run a check.

"I thought you'd bought it," Scanner said to Maro. They stood in the shade of the cafeteria annex, along with Raze and Chameleon. Sandoz was within earshot, but far enough away to seem to be standing alone.

"I thought so myself, for a while," Maro said. "It worked, but not quite as well as I'd hoped." He explained, also telling them about Berque. They listened carefully.

"So, does that mean we go or not?" Raze asked.

"Yeah," Chameleon put in, "it sounds like Deltian roulette, with full charges."

"We still go. It makes it tougher, because I can't come

to every cell to get you, but I've got some ideas about that. I can get out of my cell, and if we work it right, you'll all be in one place so I can collect you."

"How do you plan to manage that?" Sandoz said, his voice pitched just high enough to carry to them.

Maro grinned. "You are all going to get sick after lunch. So are about twenty other prisoners."

"What are you talking about?" This from Raze.

"Food poisoning," Maro replied. "Somebody cooked a bad batch of something for lunch today."

"What about Berque?" Scanner asked. "I trust him as far as I can fly naked through hyperspace."

"We don't have much choice. Somebody needs to stay with him every minute, in case he decides he'd rather make points with the warden than risk his neck with us."

"Where is he now?" Sandoz asked.

"Sick bay. I've got Fish watching him."

Raze said, "That's a lot like asking a wolf to watch a hyena."

"Fish wants out and Berque might screw it up," Maro said. "If Berque bats an eye at a guard, Fish will kill them both. And Berque knows it."

Chameleon shuddered. "Fish is crazy. I don't trust him, either."

"We don't want too many of us getting sick at lunch," Maro said. "That's two less, since they're already there."

Silence followed. Nobody looked particularly happy about Berque and Fish, but like Maro said, there was nothing to be done about it.

"I'm glad for you," Juete said into her com. Inside, she felt cold. He would be leaving, and she would not.

"I've gotten Scanner to pinpoint your location," Maro said. "I know where you are. There's only one guard to the isolation cells."

"I appreciate it, Dain, but the risk—"

"—is one I'm willing to take. I'll come for you, Juete. Be ready."

"Dain, you don't have to—"

"Hey, it isn't up for debate. You go. Period."

In her cell, Juete smiled, despite the tears that had started to flow. He was coming for her. That meant something, even if they failed. It meant a lot.

The emetic was easy enough. It wasn't a drug likely to be abused much, and the inmate medtech also owed Scanner a favor, which made it easier still. A deal was made, barter was done, and the tech had a one-shot hall pass straight from the computer, issued courtesy of Scanner.

Maro dusted one tray of a bean salad while Sandoz distracted the server. If the man noticed, he didn't say anything. The members of the escape group all took servings of the salad, though all were careful to stir it around and not eat any of it. The drug was harmless in itself, but its consequences were not pleasant to experience.

An hour after lunch, the first prisoners began vomiting. Food poisoning was relatively rare, but it had happened enough so that the guards thought they knew what was happening. Thirty-two prisoners were admitted to the infirmary for treatment, including Raze, Scanner, Chameleon and Sandoz. Most of the sick inmates were released, but a dozen of them seemed ill enough to remain overnight. Only six of them really were.

Maro returned to his cell in the late afternoon. Three cells away, a brace of guards were tearing up a mattress, searching for contraband. A sweep. Maro's gut twisted. There was no place to hide the DM gear, and no way to get it out without being seen. They were dead.

Then he noticed that Parker was the supervising guard. A desperate plan occurred to Maro.

"Officer Parker? Could I talk to you a moment?"

The guard looked up in annoyance. "What is it, pinhead?"

"It's, uh, private."

Parker looked at the other guards, who were busy in the cell, then back at Maro. He moved closer. "What?"

"You know that, uh, *device* that Scanner is building for you?"

Parker glanced back at the other guards. When he spoke again, it was in a lowered tone. "Yeah? What about it?"

"It's stashed in my cell. These guys find it, they'll confiscate it, won't they?"

Parker chewed on that for a second. "Yeah. Damn."

"Look, I'm not hiding anything else. Why don't you come on over and search. That way, you can tell them you've checked it and we can keep the thing for you until we get it running right."

Parker looked at the other guards. "Yeah. Not a bad idea." Louder, he said, "I'm gonna go ahead and search a couple more. Keep on doing what you're doing."

In Maro's cell, Parker hefted the DM unit and the confounder. "This it?"

"Yes." God, he hoped the man didn't know anything about electronics . . .

Parker stared at it. "Kinda small, ain't it?"

Maro let out a slow breath. "Yes. Scanner knew you'd want to keep it out of sight, so he made it especially small."

Parker said, "It working enough so I can see anything yet?"

"No. Scanner says by tomorrow."

Park grinned. "Good." He shoved the two pieces back into Maro's mattress, then did a quick search of the rest of the cell. "You keep your mouth shut about this, you hear?" he told Maro.

"Yes, sir."

When the other guards came to Maro's cell, Parker

waved them on. "I checked it already. It's clean." When he passed, he gave Maro a tight grin. Maro nodded slightly and held his breath until they started on the next cell.

It took a long time for his stomach to calm down.

"Here's the report on the search, Warden."

Stark looked up at Lepto and the flatscreen the big guard held. "Is it in the computer?"

"Yes, sir."

"Fine. Anything interesting?"

"Some locally grown leaf in a couple of cells, a knife made from a spring, a couple of cans of geltrol with cloth fuses, ten or twelve bottles of potato brew."

"That's it?"

"Yes, sir."

"Okay. Throw the knifer and geltrols into the holes. Find out from the dopers and drinkers where the patch and still are, then stick them in solitary, too. Use *C* wing."

"I think that *B* wing has all the cells open—"

"I said *C* wing."

Lepto nodded impassively. "Yes, sir."

After Lepto had left, Stark punched up the search report and studied it. If anything, there was less contraband than usual. Once he'd found a working laser, built from a sheet metal cutter, and once before that a thermite bomb big enough to take out a whole cell block. This time it was almost disappointing. He had been so sure that something major would turn up, and nothing had. Ah, well. So much the better, actually; he had enough problems to deal with. His line to Maro was in the infirmary with some kind of infection, and there were still a dozen prisoners with gut-rot from the bad salad at lunch. Damn, it never rained but it poured.

And at that thought, the first distant thunder reached him, as the almost-like-clockwork afternoon electrical storm rolled toward the Cage. Stark relaxed, leaning back in his chair. Things would settle down tomorrow, after Karnaaj worked on Maro and left. He was sure he could steal some of that bastard's thunder with what Berque had learned. It would have to do, although the idea of mindwiping Maro still held some appeal.

He glanced at his desk chronometer. Time to go and visit Juete, and to hell with all this crap. Maybe he would sleep with her tonight, since Karnaaj wasn't coming until the morning. That should make her happy . . .

The night deepened, and Maro tried to rest, but even the relaxation techniques he had learned so well did not help; he could only lay there nervously, his heart pounding and his mouth dry, waiting for the time. There was a shift change at midnight, and he was set to go at one. Time enough for the new shift to settle down, they had figured. There was no way to know how long it would take for him to get to the infirmary. And he hadn't told them about Juete.

If they were lucky, they might have four hours of head start before the morning count, and if everything went right, four hours would put them out of reach. If Scanner managed to kill the comnet like he said he could, and if they could circumvent the locks on the warden's personal skimmer and get clear without being been, and if—*if, if, if*.

No point in worrying about it now.

He clutched the DM in sweaty hands, waiting as the time dragged slowly by. Finally, the moment came. He was five minutes early when he started the DM, but he couldn't wait any longer. Five minutes wouldn't make any difference, and if he had to lie still for another second he would go crazy.

He had eight-seven percent power; less than the last time, and there was more than a little reason to worry that they'd run out of juice before moving eight people through enough Zonn walls to get to the skimmer. But again, there was nothing to be done for it.

Maro took a deep breath, pointed the device at the rear wall of his cell, and triggered it. The wall turned to fluid as it had before, and, pulse racing, Maro again stepped into another dimension.

∗ fifteen ∗

Stark stormed out of Juete's cell in a rage. *Damn* her! How could she run so hot and cold? She was either all over him, begging him to stay, or she acted as if being with him was the most boring thing in the galaxy! Oh, she went through the moves, even seemed to enjoy it—but that was her genetic programming, no more. He could tell the difference. It was like the first few times all over again, and he *hated* it that way. Now that he had felt her fire, nothing less would satisfy him.

Let her rot in there, then. Maybe he'd just leave her alone for a few days and see how she liked it! But even as he stalked the silent hallways, Stark knew he wouldn't do that. He *loved* her, why couldn't she see that? Somehow, someday, she *would* see it, if it took the rest of her life. He would make certain of it.

It started out lucky. Maro took five steps to his left and pointed the DM at the wall. Then he stepped through, to find himself standing in the corridor between *A* and *B* blocks. Since his cell was on the north end of *E* block, he had skipped both *D* and *A*. Juete was in *B*, and the guard at the entrance was the only one he would have to pass.

The only way he could have hit it better would have been to walk directly into her cell.

He approached the guard, who sat at a desk facing the locked door to the isolation cells. That was logical; it was unlikely that anybody would try to break *into* isolation. There were several ways to play this scenario, and Maro had decided to act as if he had a good reason for being there until he could get close enough to the man to floor him. It would be nice if the guard didn't see him until too late . . .

It would have been nice, but it wasn't going to happen that way. The guard was neither asleep nor slow in reacting. He heard Maro when the latter was ten meters away, stood and pointed a broad-beam, single-shot hand wand at the smuggler.

"Hold it. What are you doing here?"

Maro smiled and held up the DM. "A delivery for the prisoner in *B* block."

"There ain't no prisoners in *B*, buddy."

Maro nodded and gave the man a conspiratorial wink. "Right. But the warden wants you to put this in a certain cell, you copy?"

The man frowned. "I thought nobody but me and the warden knew about her being there."

"That's right. I'm only a prisoner, I don't count."

The guard nodded. "Right about that. Okay, lemme see it." He waved Maro forward.

Maro realized there was no way he was going to take the man. The guard had his hand wand carefully aimed at Maro, and with that wide aperture, it was impossible to miss.

As Maro approached, the guard reached for his com board. "I'll have to check this with the warden. Funny, he didn't say anything about it when he left here a few minutes ago . . ."

"It's a surprise," Maro said. His already dry mouth

grew yet drier. "But go ahead and check, he should be in his office by now."

The guard began to punch in the warden's personal code. It didn't matter where Stark was; if that sequence was completed, it would reach the warden. And if the guard got through to Stark, the escape was dead.

Maro sucked in a quick breath. He didn't want to do it, he wasn't even sure it would work, but he had no choice. He pointed the DM at the guard's belly and pushed the red button.

The guard screamed as his abdomen literally burst into flame, spewing entrails. He was probably dead from massive shock before he collapsed over the desk. His last living act was to trigger the hand wand, but by the time he fired the weapon, it was pointed straight up. The flash vibrated paint flakes from the ceiling, but otherwise did no harm.

Maro stared at the dead man. He had seen bodies exposed to hard vacuum through ruptured suits, and corpses bloating in the hot sunshine of a battlefield, but nothing quite so gruesome as this. The stench was almost enough to make him faint—that, coupled with the sickening realization that *he* had killed this man. Bile rose, and he turned away from the guard and vomited. It took him a minute to regain his composure; then he punched in the open code, and the door to *B* block slid back. Another touch, and all the isolation cells' doors swung open.

Juete was waiting for him. When he stepped inside, she looked at him for all of two seconds before rushing forward and embracing him. Maro felt himself respond to her, even under the circumstances.

"Come on," he said. "We've got to go."

"Thank you for coming for me."

"We'll talk about it later."

"Are you okay?"

He hesitated, then told her. "I had to kill the guard."

"That means there's no turning back."

"Yeah." He took her hand. "Come on."

He pointed the DM at the Zonn wall to the rear of her cell. "Stay close. It's very strange, where we're going."

"Don't worry. You'll have a white shadow."

Maro had to grin. He liked this woman.

His luck was not bad this time, but neither was it good. It took three tries before they reached a place where Maro felt they could risk going the rest of the way in the real world. The first time had put them outside the shop; the second in a cell in *D* block—an empty one, fortunately. The third time they found themselves in the cafeteria. At least it was in the same wing as the infirmary. With luck, nobody would be in the corridors. They'd have to pass the morgue, the zombie ward and the rec room, but there were no posted guards until the infirmary.

Maro stroked the patch on his throat. "Scanner," he said quietly.

"Yes. Where the hell are you? It's past two."

"I'll be there in exactly two minutes. Tell Sandoz."

"Copy."

To Juete he said, "Sandoz is going to distract the guard. You stay by the corner of the rec room, out of sight, until I take the guard out, okay?"

"Anything you say."

Two minutes later, in the infirmary, Maro was able to sneak up behind the guard, who was telling Sandoz to shut the fuck up, and clout him into unconsciousness. He took the single-shot wand, turned and called to Juete, then opened the locked door.

Sandoz saw the woman first. "What the hell is she doing here?"

"She's going with us."

"Bloody hell she is! She's the warden's!"

"She's *nobody's*—and she goes with us."

The two men glared at each other. Scanner broke the tension. "We don't want to stand here like a college debate team. We have to move!"

Sandoz nodded. "Yeah. We'll talk about this later, Maro."

Some of the other prisoners in the ward wondered aloud what was going on, but Sandoz turned his anger upon them. "Shut up! Some of us are leaving. The rest of you are going to take a nap, so you don't accidentally tell anybody. Chameleon!"

The polymorph moved quickly among the six other prisoners, using skin poppers on them. They were still too sick to put up more than a token resistance. Within a couple of minutes, everyone save those involved in the escape were drugged into a deep sleep.

"Okay," Maro said. "Stay close." He walked to the Zonn wall on the north end of the infirmary. The morgue was behind that wall in one world. Only the gods knew what lay behind it in another.

"Better charge the DM again," Scanner said. "We might need the power."

"Right." Maro reached down and touched the yellow button. The power diode lit and began to climb. Then, abruptly, it stopped, and the lights in the infirmary flickered momentarily. When they steadied again, they were dimmer.

Scanner cursed. "I think we blew a station on the broadcast grid. The Cage's backup generator just kicked in. How much power do we have?"

"Seventy-two percent."

"It'll have to do. We need to go, quickly! A power failure is going to alert somebody."

"All right," Maro said to the other seven prisoners surrounding him. "Stay close to each other and to me. The Zonn world isn't like this one, and I don't want anybody wandering off. When one of us goes through, we all go through, fast—otherwise we might wind up in different places. Ready?''

He looked at the others: Juete, Sandoz, Scanner, Raze, Chameleon, Fish and Berque. Only the latter two looked markedly frightened. Once again, Maro wished they weren't going along. ''Okay. Let's do it.''

Whatever luck he'd had with his travels in the Zonn realm before left him this time. Maro led the escapees through four times, and four times they had to retreat back into the wall from such places as the kitchen, the library, the Zonn Chamber and *F* block. Fortunately, they were not seen. But that was the extent of their luck—the power levels were down to fifteen percent. Barely enough for one more try, Scanner figured.

Once more in the eerie world constructed by the Zonn, Maro said, ''Okay, this is it. Wherever we come out this time, we go it on foot from there. If you have gods, pray to them that we don't come out outside the wall.''

Maro triggered the DM for the last time, and the eight of them hustled through, and into—

''Ah, shit,'' Chameleon said. ''I've worked in here before. It's the guard's quarters. The goddamned showers in the guard's quarters. How are we gonna get out of here?''

It was Raze who offered an answer. ''There's a window,'' she said, pointing. ''Up there.''

''It's barred, Raze,'' Fish said. ''You blind?''

Raze glared down at him. ''Boost me up,'' she told Sandoz and Maro. The two men lifted her. The window was wide enough for Raze to sit on the sill and prop her boots against one of the bars while she gripped the one next to it with both hands.

Maro looked away from Raze to see Berque stroking Juete's back with one sweaty hand. The woman slapped his hand away sharply, but Berque only grinned. He kept his distance, though, especially after locking gazes with Maro.

In the window, Raze flexed and began to work the bars. She shoved and pulled; muscles bulged and sweat beaded on her bare arms. Very quickly, the metal began to move. It took maybe ten seconds before there was a gap wide enough to allow passage. Raze grinned down at the others. "Everybody up."

One by one they made their way between the stretched bars and out of the shower room. Maro was the last, aided up by Sandoz.

Outside, the early morning air was still and warm. Insects swarmed around the big HT lights, shadows dancing across the pooled beams in the yard. The transportation shack was behind an electric fence a hundred meters to the southeast of the guards' quarters. It was almost 0300, and they were behind schedule.

There were three guards patrolling the fence, and no way to cross that patch of well-lit ground between the guards' quarters and the fence without being seen by the west side guard.

"It's up to you," Maro told Chameleon.

"Don't I know it," the mue said.

"Can you do it? Are you sure?"

"I'm the best there is at this. If I can't, nobody can."

Chameleon began to change. His face shifted, his hair changed texture and color, and, after three minutes, he was a passable clone of Warden Stark, at least in the dark. He slipped into the coverall that Sandoz shoved at him, and Juete gasped.

"Looks pretty good, doesn't it?" Chameleon said.

"As long as you keep your mouth shut," Sandoz replied.

Maro pulled the hand wand he'd taken from the guard and offered it to Chameleon. "You want to take this?"

"No, thanks. If I use it, the others will see the flash. I'll do it the hard way."

"Good luck."

"Right."

They watched as the altered Chameleon strolled across the lighted compound. The guard spotted him and spun around, pointing his shotgun. Chameleon kept walking. Maro rubbed his palms against his pants. The guard straightened slightly. He lowered the shotgun and said something, but Maro couldn't make it out. Chameleon kept walking.

When the two men were only a few meters apart, Chameleon suddenly pointed at a spot behind the guard and spoke. Again, the escapees could not make out the words. The guard turned away, raising the shotgun. Chameleon pulled a cosh that Sandoz had given him from his pocket and clouted the guard with it. The man went down.

"Okay, move!" Maro hissed.

The seven of them sprinted across the well-lit grass. Raze was in front, Maro and Sandoz just behind her, with the others strung out behind them. Chameleon bent and retrieved the fallen guard's shotgun, then began moving along the fence as if patrolling.

Raze reached the unconscious guard and picked him up, carrying him close to the electric fence. The other guards couldn't see them, but anybody to the north or west could if they looked. They had to hurry.

Sandoz bent over the guard. "A spetsdöd!" Quickly he peeled up the plastic flesh that attached the dart gun to the back of the guard's hand. In another five seconds he had mounted the weapon on his own hand.

"The light!" Maro said.

Sandoz looked up. "He's loading shocktox. The darts might not break the glass."

"Try!"

Sandoz raised the spetsdöd and touched the barrel with his finger. There came a series of hard coughs; the hail of darts rattled against the HT lamp's glass. The cover chipped, starred, then cracked. The spetsdöd's cough stopped.

"Damn!" Sandoz ejected the empty magazine and rummaged around in the guard's belt pouch. He found a spare magazine and fitted it, then began firing again. After three seconds, the glass shattered and the bulb blew out. Darkness fell on them like a curtain.

"Okay, Scanner."

Scanner took a fist-sized plastic block from his pocket. He touched a control on the device, which gave off a quick sparkle of LEDs. Then he moved to the three-meter-tall diamond mesh fence and gingerly touched the thing to the thick wire. A spark jumped.

Scanner took a quick breath, then reached out and grabbed the fence next to the mechanism. Nothing happened. He grinned. "It's working. We should have a ten-meter-wide patch recircuited."

"Go," Maro said. "Hurry!"

They began to climb the fence.

In his cube, Stark was restless. Another goddamned power failure had just been reported. He paced back and forth in front of the south window, noticing that one of the lamps on the transportation area fence was out as well. Goddamned place was falling apart. Who the hell was on guard detail down there? Lepto was running the unit tonight, wasn't he? He must be on the opposite side. Lepto would never let a light go out on him for more than the time it took to roust a tech out of bed to fix it.

Stark turned away from the window to his desk and stroked a heat-sensitive strip. "Get me tower two," he said.

"There, next to that bus!" Scanner pointed.

Their target was Stark's personal flitter. It was an aircar that would comfortably seat six, and uncomfortably eight.

Comfort was not a problem; they would fly standing on their heads if that was what it took.

"I hope this works," Chameleon said.

"It'll work," Scanner replied, pulling another electronic device from his pocket. "I've had this for two years, just in case I ever got a chance to use it. I know the control systems of this cart better than my mother's face. It'll work."

They reached the flitter. Scanner tapped in a code on his device, the doors on the flitter gulled up and open. "See?"

"Brag later," Sandoz said. "Let's get the fuck out of here."

"Everybody freeze!"

Maro spun tightly, pointing the hand wand. To his left, he saw Sandoz drop flat to the ground, spetsdöd extended. Chameleon moved slower, bringing the shotgun around.

A laser dot danced across Fish's chest, and the little man erupted in a fountain of bloody flesh. Fish screamed and bounced from the side of the flitter, falling.

The shotgun's flash came from the edge of a second transport bus. Maro pointed the hand wand at the after-image and triggered it. The strobe-like flash spread out, too wide and dispersed to do much damage at that range. He tossed the one-shot weapon away as he heard the rattle of spetsdöd darts against the bus's plastic body. Chameleon got his shotgun working, and three quick booms deafened Maro. "Into the flitter!" he yelled into the sudden silence. Berque scrambled inside, followed by Juete. Maro looked up to see Raze running to the right, sprinting. Where the hell was she going? Wait, she was circling the bus—

The dot of the targeting laser whipped over Maro, and he dove for the ground. The hail of 9mm pellets sleeted against the flitter. Sandoz fired the spetsdöd again, then cursed as the weapon ran dry. He jerked it from his hand, jumped up and into a dive, and rolled toward the flitter.

Chameleon beat Sandoz to the door.

"The shotgun!" Maro yelled. Chameleon turned and tossed the weapon at Maro. Maro caught it and rolled, then came up.

By the bus, somebody grunted.

Maro ran toward the bus, shotgun pointed ahead. He waited for the deadly red spot to find him, for the impact of the steel shot to slam into him. It didn't come.

Somebody was fighting behind the bus. Maro skidded to a halt on the rough plastcrete slab and gathered himself to spring. Before he could move, the fighters bounced from behind the bus and almost on top of him, clinched together like wrestlers.

It was Raze, locked together with Lepto. The guard cursed, while Raze saved her breath for fighting. As he watched, they sprang apart. Then Lepto moved in, and Raze swung a roundhouse punch, bringing it up from behind her, a long, looping and powerful strike. It caught Lepto flush on the side of the jaw. Maro heard the bone go with a wet snap, and Lepto's head jerked to the side from the power of the strike. That punch might have badly injured an ordinary man, but Lepto only stopped long enough to shake his head before he started for Raze again.

Maro remembered the guard he had killed, and that was enough to make him lower the barrel of the shotgun to point at Lepto's legs. He fired, and the blast hit the guard above the left knee, knocking the leg back enough to pitch Lepto forward in a hard dive. Raze danced to the side as the guard hit the plastcrete. He might bleed to death eventually, but he was alive for now.

"Come on!" Maro yelled to Raze.

Raze hesitated, fists doubled, staring at Lepto. Then she turned and ran.

The two of them piled into the flitter. Sirens wailed, and spotlights came on, but nobody seemed to know where to focus yet.

Scanner sat in the control seat, holding a small caster in

one hand. He thumbed the unit's control and tossed it onto the flitter's dash panel. "There goes the comnet and radio," he said. "They won't be calling for help for a few hours."

"Get this thing in the air," Sandoz said.

Scanner nodded and powered up the flitter. In five seconds, the craft started to lift.

"All right!" Chameleon said.

The plastic window next to Juete shattered. She screamed as the shards exploded inward. Maro jumped for her, pulling her away from the window. There was a rattle like hail against the flitter's body, and the sounds of gunfire. He caught a glimpse of Lepto, sprawled on the plastcrete, firing at them with his recovered shotgun. He jammed his own weapon through the vacant window, pointed it at Lepto, and pulled the trigger back to full auto.

On the plastcrete, Lepto's form jerked from the impact. The shotgun emptied and clicked, and Maro shoved it outside. The flitter rose as Maro turned to look at Juete. A line of blood, startlingly vivid against her white flesh, ran down one cheek.

"I'm okay," she said. "Just some plastic hit me, I think."

The flitter canted, then began to move, picking up speed, heading through the transport area toward the southern wall. Maro looked out through the ruined window as the wall seemed to drop away beneath them.

"We're out," Raze said quietly.

They all yelled, then. A cheer.

They had escaped from the Omega Cage.

* Part Two *

"Freedom don't mean much when the dogs is on your trail."

—Abraham Scranton Jefferson Jones

* sixteen *

''We're losing power,'' Scanner said.

A chorus of voices was raised in immediate and shocked question. In reply, Scanner shook his head and pointed to the readouts on the heads-up holodisplay. ''One of Lepto's shotgun blasts. This thing's diagnostics show that we're losing fuel—a ruptured line.''

''Can we fix it?'' Sandoz asked.

''Not without landing. Maybe not even then. I've got a confounder blasting their radar and doppler, but I don't think we want to put down within a hundred klicks of the prison. They can still field dins and hounds, and they have other transports. We can't hide our heat shadow.''

''Shit,'' Chameleon commented. He had shifted back from his Stark impersonation to what Maro assumed was his normal appearance, if indeed he had any.

''How long can we fly?'' Maro asked.

Scanner shrugged. ''If we keep our speed low and stay low, out of turbulence, maybe a couple of hours.''

''How far?'' Raze asked.

''Three, four hundred kilometers.''

''That puts us six hundred short of the mining port,'' Berque said bitterly. ''We're dead.''

"Maybe," Maro said.

Berque stared at Maro as if he had just sprouted tentacles and green fur. " 'Maybe'? How the hell are we supposed to get through six hundred kilometers of some of the deadliest animal and plant life in the whole fucking galaxy? Walk?"

"Unless you've got a better idea."

Berque looked at the others. "Yeah, I have a better idea! We go back! So we have to do some time in the hole, that's better than dying! Stark isn't so bad—"

Raze was covering the shattered window with a seat cushion. She easily twisted a thick piece of metal frame out of the way so it could fit, jammed it into place, then turned and smiled at Berque. "Shut up," she said softly.

Berque shut up.

To Maro, Raze said, "Can we make it on foot?"

Maro said, "Scanner has the map."

Scanner tapped his head and grinned. "Right in here."

Maro looked at the others. "Anybody else want to go back? It's true that we might die on the surface. It's a risk."

Chameleon shook his head; Juete hers; Sandoz only grinned. Maro said, "Scanner?"

"I'm with you."

Maro nodded. "Okay, we go. You can stay with the flitter when we put down if you want, Berque. I expect they'll find you quickly enough."

Berque licked his lips. "Ah, maybe I'd better stay with you."

Maro turned back to Scanner. "Okay, see how long you can keep this crippled bird up."

"Copy that."

Slowly, the wounded flitter flew on through the night.

Stark was filled with both rage and fear. He held himself as calmly as he could as he listened to the reports pouring from all over the prison.

"Lepto is dead, shot . . ."

"Your personal flitter is gone, but we've got positive indications of a fuel leak . . ."

"Radar is showing funny signals, and doppler is worse . . ."

"The main transceiver is down, and we don't know why . . ."

"Enough," Stark said. "Put cycles in the air, standard search grid. They've got some kind of jammer—triangulate on the interference. I want ground cars out, headed toward Omega City and the mines. Start up the infrared. Put a hound on the flitter's fuel."

A guard appeared on the flatscreen monitor. "What about a messenger to the city? Cut 'em off on the other end."

"No. We take care of our own problems here. Discom."

Stark severed the com link, then stood and paced to the window. The last thing he wanted to do was let anybody in the city know about the escape. That would be all Karnaaj would need, some indication of ineptitude. As it stood, so long as the radio was out, nobody would be running any shuttles to the Cage from Omega City. That would keep Karnaaj off his back for a couple of days. Of course, they would eventually send a messenger out to see what was going on, but Stark could put a hold on him too, in the interests of prison security. A few days was all he needed; by then he'd have the escapees back.

"Computer, list the prisoners missing from their cells."

Obediently, the computer lit with the names. Eight of them, he saw, counting the one Lepto got at the M&T yard.

And Juete.

Their escape didn't frighten him; what did was the worry that by the time his men got to them, there might not be much left of those seven fools who had hopped the wall. Omega was as dangerous as an Earth-class planet could be, even to people armed with state-of-the-art technology. If their ship was damaged, they would have to land, and for a handful of ill-equipped prisoners on foot, Omega would provide a fast grave.

He didn't need that. He *had* to save Juete. The bitch! How could she have *done* this to him? Hadn't he done *everything* for her? She'd be sorry when he caught her.

And Maro. If Karnaaj was pissed about being kept away for a few days, it would be nothing compared to what he would feel if Maro died a hundred klicks away from the Cage. No, he had to get them back, and fast.

If worse came to worse, there was the Juggernaut. He didn't want to use it unless he had to—it was his final ace, and once it was played there would be hell to pay. He was not supposed to have the thing. Aside from being paid for out of stolen funds, he had bought the military machine from black market sources. The Confed would burn his shadow into a wall if they found out about the Juggernaut.

Still, it was there if he had to use it, and the thought gave him some comfort, however small.

Far better, however, that his men should catch up to the escapees on their own. And quickly.

Juete turned away from the other passengers in the flitter to stare through the polarized window at the desolate landscape. The dawn spread its reddish glow over the terrain, illuminating a vast expanse of desert. Far to the south and below them, she thought she saw a dragonbat gliding.

She tried to maintain her calm. Long ago, the albino Exotics had discovered that becoming excited only made them more desirable; it stirred hormones and sent out potent signals. Already she could feel the lust focusing upon her from the others in the confines of the small craft. Berque was the most open about it, but it also came in various degrees from all the others, even Dain.

Given the circumstances, it was impossible to meditate, to achieve that single-pointedness that helped to cool her normal pheromonic heat; still, watching the sand and scrub pass close beneath her helped somewhat.

Berque moved to stand next to her seat. He rubbed his palms against his coveralls, leaving damp sweat tracks. "Hey, what say you and I go in the back for a few minutes?"

She turned to look up at him. "No."

"Come on." His voice was hoarse. "You're an Exotic, you like it."

"I choose my partners."

"What's wrong with me?"

"Have you got a few hours for a basic list?"

"Berque." The summons came from Maro, who turned from where he squatted next to Scanner. The fat man glanced at the smuggler. "Yeah?"

"Go sit down." His voice was flat, yet somehow frightening.

For a beat, it looked as if Berque might protest. Whatever he thought, however, he kept to himself, turned and moved back to his seat.

Juete smiled at Maro, who nodded slightly and returned to whatever he and Scanner had been discussing. The albino woman leaned back against her seat and stared through the window. The thought of being with Dain made her heart begin to race, and she didn't want to start producing chemical signals that might excite the others. The trick was to keep those who wanted her from becoming so possessive that they would be willing to kill to keep her. Or even to kill *her* to keep others from having her. Berque was disgusting, but she had been with worse and survived. If he had a weapon, she would do as he wished, to keep him from killing her or the others.

Fortunately, he was not in charge. It was always a value decision, and sex *per se* was not worth much to her compared to respect, compared to love. Now that she had that, she could be choosier.

The flitter seemed to cough. It bucked once, slowed, then picked up speed again. Juete looked at Scanner.

Without looking away from the bug-streaked windscreen, Scanner said, "We've got about twenty minutes of fuel left. I'm going to look for a place to land."

Outside, the desert came to an end. Just beyond stood a small range of hills, and past that a deep, wide crevasse split the ground, running toward the horizon until it disappeared into a thin line. Scanner found a passage through the hills without climbing. Once they passed over the crevasse the terrain changed abruptly, turning, as if by some mad terraformer's design, into a swamp. Tall trees reared up from boggy ground and large patches of scummy water were broken up by clumps of vegetation in a dozen shades of green.

"I can't understand how the geology of this place functions," she heard Dain mutter to Scanner. The circuit-rider replied. "Neither does anyone else. They think it has to do with some planetary engineering conducted by the Zonn."

For another fifteen minutes they cruised at just above treetop height over the swamp. Then the flitter started to cough again, sputtering and shuddering this time.

"I don't want to cut it too close," Scanner said. "There's a clear patch just ahead that's big enough to set down in but not so big as to be real obvious to a search from the air. "Strap in."

Juete pulled her seat harness tight and locked the plastic snaps together. Dain moved down the aisle and sat next to her. He put his own harness on, then caught her hand in his own, squeezing it lightly. She smiled nervously at him.

"It'll be okay," he said.

"I know. Thank you."

* * *

Scanner did a slick job putting the flitter down. The engines cut out again when they had almost landed, perhaps a meter up, and the craft hit the boggy ground solidly, but not hard enough to do more than jar everybody.

"Welcome to the scenic Omega wetlands," Scanner said. "Please keep off the grass and do not feed the animals."

"Funny," Chameleon said. "You should be on the vids."

Maro stood. "Okay, we need to gather whatever supplies this thing has and get moving."

Raze stood in a finely tuned athletic motion. "Should we cover the flitter with branches or something?"

Scanner laughed. "If they get close enough to see the ship, they'll pick up the heat shadow on their scopes. Might as well save ourselves some work. Besides, who cares if they find the flitter? They won't know which way we went."

"They'll know where we started," Sandoz said. "They'll grid from here."

"Why don't we blow it up?" Berque said.

"And leave a nice bright beacon leading to us?" Sandoz replied. "No. Maro is right. Let's just get the hell out of here."

Maro had already moved to the supply locker, which he opened. Not too bad. There was an emergency radio transceiver, a week's worth of concentrates for three people, an electromagnetic compass/line-of-sight distance laser, a four-shot flare pistol with a dozen signal flares, three bottles of water and a blister pack of purification tabs; a first-aid kit, three blankets and three bottles of insect repellent, and a fat tube of sunblock cream. All of it would fit neatly into two back packs, which had been thoughtfully included. It could be far worse. Pity there were no weapons save for the flare gun—but it was better than nothing. Maro stuck it in his pocket, along with the extra flares, and began to load the other supplies into the packs.

"Heysoo, it's *hot* already out there!" That from Chameleon, who stood in the doorway as the hatch gulled upward. "Makes the Cage seem air conditioned!"

"Get used to it," Scanner said. "This swamp goes on for at least another thirty klicks in any direction you pick."

"Great," Chameleon replied. "I wonder if I can turn into a lizard?"

"How would we know if you did?" Raze said, smiling.

"Oh, funny. You and Scanner, you should form a comedy team. Beauty and the beast, and you can pick which is which."

Maro tossed the sunblock to Juete and one of the bottles of insect repellant to Sandoz. "Let's move, people. Coat up with bug cream. There's lots of shade, but we won't be able to hide from the insects like we can the sunshine." He shouldered one of the packs and handed the other to Raze. He smiled at Juete, who was rubbing the sunblock onto her skin with practiced motions, and then walked to the door. He stepped out into the hard shade of the tropical swamp, and the heat fell on him like a wet sheet. The air was alive with the hum of insects, and a slight breeze carried more damp heat and the stench of rotting vegetation.

Something unseen chittered angrily behind a screen of man-high bushes a dozen meters to his left. It was not a landscape he had ever experienced before, but now there was no choice. Maro stepped down onto the ground, sinking a centimeter into the springy humus, and turned to look at the others gathering in the doorway of the flitter.

"Come on," he said. "It isn't going to get any better if you wait."

Silently, they all filed out into the swamp.

✳ seventeen ✳

The beasts of the swamp were not so much large and dangerous as they were everywhere. The operative mode of the animals seemed to be that, if they saw something larger than themselves, they ran; if it was smaller than they were, they ate it. If there were any plant eaters—and there had to be—Maro hadn't seen them.

"Here come the birds!" Sandoz said.

Maro pulled the flare pistol and squatted. The others dropped to the mushy ground as a flock of screeching bloodbirds fluttered through the trees. Twice before, this or a similar collection had dived at the escapees. The bloodbirds weren't very big; their wingspan was about the size of a man's hands, but they carried a lot of tiny sharp teeth in their bills. The first pass had resulted in several small but painful bites for Maro, Berque and Chameleon. The second time, the flock had occupied a tree for a minute before diving. This time, Maro was going to be ready.

The bloodbirds settled into a tree just ahead. Before they could gather themselves for their attack, Maro raised the flare pistol and fired one of the star-burst flares at the tree.

He aimed at the trunk, high up, so the flare wouldn't sail past harmlessly.

The flare hit the tree and stuck just below a major bifurcation. A couple of the bloodbirds took wing, a few more shifted a little, but the rest took no apparent notice as the small red fire burned brightly against the tree. Then, suddenly, the flare burst, sending a hot red shower through the branches of the bloodbirds' haven, hundreds of tiny spears lancing through the leaves.

It was a gratifying sight. Dozens of leaves caught fire, and a handful of bloodbirds left smoking trails as the flock scattered in primal fear, screaming. If there remained any interest in feeding on the seven below, there was no evidence of it.

Sandoz laughed. "Nice shot. The little fuckers won't bother us for a while, I'd guess."

"Owch! Shit!"

They turned to see Chameleon dancing around, rubbing at one arm. Several small punctures on the flesh were already red and swelling. Maro glanced down to see an innocuous plant that the face-dancer had crushed when he'd dropped to avoid the bloodbirds. A sharp and bitter scent filled the air.

"Some kind of poison," Raze said.

Maro already had the first-aid kit out. He pulled the small flatscreen from its niche and punched in a description of the plant. After a few seconds the screen lit with a picture, name and short biological background on it. A stinging nettle of some sort, painful but not fatal. Maro read the treatment, selected a popper from the kit and pressed the compressed-gas hypo against Chameleon's shoulder. The single shot unit popped and injected the chem into the muscle.

"Damn, it *itches!*"

"Supposed to," Maro said. "It'll neutralize the poison.

Says here it takes a day for the swelling to subside, but you'll be okay."

"Maybe we ought to spend a few minutes reading that thing," Juete said, pointing at the flatscreen.

"Tonight," Maro replied. "For now, let's keep moving and be careful not to touch anything we don't know for sure is safe."

"That doesn't leave much," Berque said, rubbing at one of the bird bites on his shoulder.

"Like I said, we move carefully."

"Which way?" Sandoz asked.

Maro lifted the laser-compass. "The port is that way." He pointed to his left.

"How far is it?" Raze asked.

"Only about five hundred and fifty kilometers," Scanner said. "Give or take fifty."

"Great," Chameleon said. "A walk in the country."

"Let's move," Maro said. He started to walk.

"Hold it," Sandoz said. "You said the port is that way." He pointed at a right angle to Maro's intended direction of travel.

"Right. But they'll be looking for us in that direction."

"How the hell else are we supposed to get off this goddamned planet if we don't go to the port?" Berque cut in.

"Oh, we're going to the port. Eventually. But there's a stop we need to make first."

With that cryptic statement hanging in the air, Maro moved off through the swamp. After a moment, the others followed.

"Show me," Stark said into his transceiver.

The airhounds were man-sized cylinders, rounded on the front and tapered to a set of vertical fins and a wide fluke at the rear. Mounted amidships on each was a sensor package that included a photomutable gel camera set to scan from UV to infrared; a specific-molecule sensor that could be locked onto any of a hundred target scents; and a shotgun bundle microphone sensitive enough to pick up a man's cough at two klicks. The repellor motors gave the things fair speed, and it had only taken seven hours for the first pair to locate the stolen flitter.

Stark saw the camera feed from the hound on his monitor. In the background, the second hound floated sedately, bobbing slightly as the repellor field adjusted itself for heat and local field fluctuation. In the foreground squatted the warden's personal flitter, sunk slightly into the soft ground.

"Set the hounds for the scent and turn them loose," Stark ordered.

Came the voice of the new head guard: "We tried that, Warden. They just whirr and click a few times, and nothing happens."

Stark clenched his fists but kept his face as emotionless as he could for the camera projecting his image to the men in the swamp. Damn, that had to be Scanner's doing. Had he tampered with the hounds before the escape? Or did he have some kind of jammer with him?

"All right, there's a malfunction. Have maintenance work on them. Meanwhile, set up a cone grid on a straight line to the mining port. Twenty degrees, squeeze at two klicks, and repeat."

"Copy that, Warden."

"And put a cycle on zig-zag on the remaining three-forty for a fifty-klick back line."

In the background, Stark saw a tech approach the hound. The man lifted a cover plate on the unit and began examining circuitry.

"Uh, begging your pardon, Warden, but that'll take forever. Besides, if they ain't headed toward the port, they won't last more'n a week—"

"That's the point. I want them alive."

The sound of shotguns reached him then, five or six blasts on full auto. "What was that?"

"Nothing. A pack of shrats nosing around."

"Get moving," Stark said. "They're only four or five hours ahead. On foot, in that swamp, they can't be more than ten or fifteen kilometers from you."

The tech working on the hound cut into the circuit. "I think I found the problem," he said. "There's a wire that doesn't belong here, and I think it's shorting out the organic molecule reader."

Stark had a sudden premonition. "Wait," he said. "Don't—!"

Too late. The screen washed out in a flare of white and the sound of the explosion funneled through the second hound into Stark's transceiver, overloading the speaker and tripping the breaker. Stark toggled the switch, and the sound cut back in.

Men screaming. He dialed the sound down. The muted yells sounded no less horrible.

Dammit! The hounds were rigged with bombs! What other little presents had they left for him?

Juete was hot and tired, and her feet and legs were sore. Even though she walked between Dain and Raze and therefore was not taking the brunt of the vines and branches that slapped at them, she still carried a dozen small scratches.

There came the sound of a distant explosion. Even in the relatively quiet jungle, the noise seemed a long way off. Dain stopped, as did the others.

"Sounds like somebody tried to fix one of the hounds," Scanner said. Berque chuckled, but nobody else laughed.

They resumed their walk. Dain, Sandoz and Raze had been taking turns breaking the trail, hacking at vegetation they couldn't go around with a crude machete Sandoz had made from a strip of metal and insulation from the flitter. It wasn't very efficient, but it was better than nothing.

"Hold it," Sandoz said quietly.

Everybody froze.

To Juete's right, something moved in the brush. It wasn't close, but it seemed to be making a lot of noise, whatever it was.

"What do you think?" Dain said to Sandoz.

"I don't know," Sandoz said. "Dogs, maybe."

"They'd have come for us already," Scanner said.

"Shrats, then. Or something we've never seen before," Sandoz said. He looked at Dain. "You'd better get that flare pistol out."

But Dain had already handed the make-shift machete to Raze and drawn the pistol.

The sound in the bushes stopped.

"We'd better find a clearing," Dain said.

"Copy that," Chameleon said. "Let's move."

Raze took the point, swiping at the vines. After another hundred meters, Dain waved everybody to a halt again. Whatever was stalking them moved for another few seconds, then stopped.

"Staying right with us," Chameleon observed.

"It's getting closer," Juete said.

"Heysoo bloody Kreesto," Sandoz said.

They moved. Ten minutes later they found a clearing. It was maybe twenty meters across, with nothing but a few vines tangled over the ground. Dain led them to the middle.

After a minute or so, the things that stalked them began to appear at the edge of the clearing.

They were ugly, Juete saw. Short, squat and ugly, about the size of a large dog, but more piglike in appearance. The beasts had furry bodies, hooved feet, and lots of teeth, mostly pointed. They didn't make any sounds, but scooted back and forth along the edge of the clearing, watching the people intently. There were about a dozen of them.

Scanner snorted. "*Schweinhunds*," he said. "Pig-dogs."

Raze hefted the machete and Dain held the flare pistol pointed in the schweinhunds' general direction. Sandoz had found a short but heavy tree branch which he held like a club. Chameleon dug through one of the packs, looking for a weapon.

Scanner glanced at him and said, "I don't think squirting them with bug repellent is going to work too well."

"I hope we go to hell together," Chameleon shot back, "so I can pound on your bloody head for a few thousand years."

"They're not attacking," Sandoz said. "It's like they want to, but they can't. Look."

Juete saw what he meant. The schweinhunds would run back and forth as though working themselves up to the point where they could charge the people, but they would take two or three hesitant steps and then back off. It happened several times.

"Maybe they're afraid of open spaces," Raze said. "Like some animals are afraid of water."

"I hope so," Dain said. "It'll be dark soon, and I don't think we can risk a fire."

A distant rumble of thunder rolled past. The hot air stirred slightly. Juete caught the scent of impending rain.

"Pretty soon," Scanner said, "I don't think we'll be able to *start* a fire."

Dain unpacked the three survival blankets. They were thin, but lined on one side with mirrored plastic to keep in body heat. "Anybody want to risk going to the opposite side of the clearing to get some branches? We can make some shelter, unless you'd rather take a shower in your clothes."

Raze started for the trees opposite the pig-dogs, and Sandoz followed her. "Hey," Dain said. Sandoz turned, and Dain tossed the flare pistol at him. Sandoz caught the weapon, spun it in his hands back and forth, and grinned.

By the time the schweinhunds caught on, Raze and Sandoz had chopped several long branches loose and were returning to the others. The wind had picked up, and the clouds had covered the sun. It took a few minutes to rig a rough cone from the wood, and they managed to tie the blankets over and around the top before the first fat drops began to pound the clearing. The schweinhunds vanished into the brush as the thunderstorm unloaded its heavy rains. The makeshift tent leaked, but it kept most of the water off. One at a time, the others stripped and went out into the rain to sluice away some of the day's sweat. Juete watched, admiring the various bodies, especially Dain's and Raze's, but she did not shower herself. No point in taking any more risks than she had to.

As night crept up on them, the storm continued. It was past dark when the rain finally stopped. The sound of water faded, and insects began to buzz as the group ate dry and nearly tasteless concentrates for their cold supper. They were tired, sore and uncomfortable, but as Juete snuggled against Dain's back, she realized that she had never been happier. They might die, but they would do it free.

✶ eighteen ✶

Berque's scream woke them.

The fat man was thrashing around, knocking the makeshift tent askew. Maro sat up, bumped into Raze's muscular back and rolled clear of the collapsing folds.

The others were also moving. Maro saw Juete's pale form in the darkness and grabbed her hand, jerking her toward him. He vaguely glimpsed somebody shifting past to his left; from the smoothness of the movement, it had to be Sandoz. Maro slapped at his hip pocket for the flare gun, but it wasn't there. He remembered then that he had given it to Sandoz earlier.

What was going on? Not even a minute had elapsed since he had been awakened by Berque's screams. The man was still screaming, a hoarse and guttural sound, and Maro couldn't see anything in the darkness.

"Sandoz! Put a flare into the ground, give us some light!"

A second later Maro heard the *pok!* of the pistol firing, and a dim red glare enveloped the clearing. The flare sputtered, illuminating a scene that could have come from some artist's conception of hell. Maro saw Chameleon first, scrambling away from the flattened tent on his hands and knees. Sandoz stood with the flare pistol, close to the guttering flare; Raze was in a fighting crouch, her arms spread, the fitful light making her look as if she were carved from iron. As he watched, Scanner scrambled out from under one of the damp blankets, got to his feet and took two steps, then tripped on a thick vine and fell flat. Maro cast a quick glance at Juete, who wore a fearful look but seemed unharmed.

Still under the collapsed tent, Berque thrashed and screamed.

Maro moved toward him, snagged his foot on another vine and fell to one knee. As he did, he felt something scrape his leg. He looked down and saw that his pants had caught on a thorn. The dying red light revealed what looked to be black fluid running from his leg. *Blood,* he thought, *it only looks black because of the light—*

Sandoz cursed. "Look at the goddamn vines! They're moving!"

Maro jumped up. The vine clung to his ankle; he kicked hard, and ripped it away. Sandoz was right, the vines *did* seem to be writhing. Not fast, like a snake, but definitely moving . . .

He leaped to the fallen tent just as Raze pulled it clear of Berque. Sandoz fired another flare. This one hit something solid and didn't sink into the ground like the first had; the light was brighter. It showed Berque, almost covered in the vines. The black liquid that Maro had seen on his leg poured from dozens of cuts and slashes on Berque's exposed body. As he watched, a thorn extruded from one of the vines like a cat's claw unsheathing and stabbed into Berque's bicep. Many of the vines' tendrils ended in suckerlike polyps that were securely fastened to the man's skin. Maro grabbed one—they were no thicker than his little finger, though they were swelling rapidly as they engorged with blood—and yanked with all his strength. He could not break its hold. Berque screamed louder.

"Help! Get them off, get them *off of me—!*"

Raze had the machete, and she chopped at the vines where they left Berque, but the things were tough. Even with her strength, only a couple of them parted. The rest showed only gouges and cuts. Blood oozed from the cut vines as it did from Berque's body.

Scanner moved in, trying to pull the living ropes away from the dying man. Maro didn't doubt that Berque was dying. The screams had grown hoarse and weaker. From the corner of his vision, Maro saw that Scanner's shoulders bore several oozing cuts as well. When he had time to notice, the smuggler found small bleeding circles on his own body.

"H-h-help . . . me . . ." Berque whispered.

They couldn't get him free, Maro realized. And, even if they could, there was no way to replace the blood he had already lost. The man's face looked like warm wax in the fading red glare, sinking in on itself. He was an organlegger and a cannibal, but even he deserved a better death than to be sucked dry by alien plants on this hellish world.

There was barely enough of the second flare's light to see when Maro turned to Raze. They exchanged quick looks. Maro glanced at the machete. Raze nodded.

She moved in and raised the machete. The flare died as the metal sang downward.

The messenger from Omega City arrived, just as Stark had expected. Stark met him in his office.

"We have an emergency," the warden said. "As of now, we are under class-one military quarantine."

"But—but—"

"Sorry. I'm invoking my authority as Sector Commander. You understand?"

"Yessir." The man took a deep breath. "I have a high-level message from Commander Karnaaj—"

"It'll have to wait. I'm in the middle of some very delicate operations."

"Sir, it's only a verbal—"

Stark jabbed his finger at the messenger's chest as though aiming a weapon. "I said it can wait. And that's the way I want your report to read, copy? You were unable to deliver Karnaaj's message upon your arrival due to a military emergency in progress."

The messenger glanced at the wall of the office, then back at Stark. The warden could almost read his mind: Cross this bastard and his ass would be skewered. Karnaaj was worse, maybe, but he was in the city and Stark was here.

The man nodded. "I copy that, Commander. Whatever you say."

Stark smiled. "Good man. One of the guards will find you a billet and get you settled in. It'll only be a few days. I'm sure you'll enjoy your stay."

When the messenger had gone, Stark turned back to his computer for an update on the hunt for the escapees. It had better be only a few days. Otherwise, it was his neck that would feel the axe.

Through the swamp they slogged, now down to six. They'd left Berque's body to the vampire vines; there was no way to bury it, and tossing it in some stagnant pool would be no better. Juete had seen three of the suckerlike abrasions clotting on her own skin when the sun had risen; all of the others also had "bites." Apparently the plant used some kind of deadening agent before locking onto a victim—she hadn't felt a thing.

They took a break two hours into the march. The sun was already raising clouds of vapor from the swamp, and the heat made Juete's temples pound. Under the sunblock, she felt hot and itchy.

"I should have known something was wrong when the

pig-dogs didn't charge,'' Sandoz said. ''I wasn't paying proper attention.''

''We didn't see it either,'' Raze said.

''That doesn't matter. In my job, if you miss a detail, it kills you.''

Juete looked at Scanner. ''I have a question.''

''Ask away.''

''The hound exploding—why didn't you just rig it to blow up at the prison? That way they couldn't have gotten so close.''

Scanner laughed. ''Good point. The problem was, I did the rigging on those beasts more than a year past. At the time I didn't think they'd be chasing a wounded flitter, homed in on the leaking fuel. I figured they'd be chasing somebody on foot.''

Raze said, ''You were planning on cutting free a year ago?''

''Not me. But I figured somebody might try it, and I just wanted to throw a break into the trackers' circuit. They run checks on the gear, but they're electronic, and the rigged hounds passed that. Once they actually started running down human scent, that was another matter.''

''Risky, when you weren't even planning on using it yourself,'' Sandoz said.

Scanner shrugged. ''One has to keep one's hand in. I didn't want to get rusty.''

''All right,'' Sandoz said. ''As long as we're playing Q and A, I got one.'' He looked at Maro. ''Why the fuck are we heading *away* from the starport at the mines? There's nothing human between us and the Roog Sea this way, and that's five thousand klicks if it's a centimeter. I went because you seemed to know what you were doing, but I want to know, too. In case you don't make it.''

Dain stretched, catlike, before he spoke. ''Once they found the flitter, there was only one way we could reasonably be headed. That's where they'll be looking. Even in the swamp, with all the animals squishing around, seven people would cast one hell of a heat-shadow. They'd spot us, very likely, unless we were in a real hot spot."

"That's only part of an answer," Chameleon said.

Dain nodded. "Right. Our chances of making it to the working mines are dirty ice. I figure the warden doesn't want anybody to know we're gone, so he probably won't set up people at the port. It'd take weeks for us to travel that far on foot, and he's got to know it. So I figure he'll comb the woods for us for a few days before he gets nervous. A week or two, at least."

Juete said, "That keeps us free for a while, but what about the long run?"

He smiled at her. "That's why we're going southeast instead of northwest. We can't make it to the port in less than a couple of weeks on foot. We need transportation."

"Is there a shuttle stop here in the swamps I haven't heard about?" Raze asked.

"Maybe. Scanner?"

Scanner looked up from rubbing his feet. "About fifty klicks further on is an abandoned mine works. It was set along the top of a half-klick-wide strip of rocky ore that runs across half the continent."

"The Granite Girdle?" Raze asked.

"You've heard of it. Well, they pulled silver and platinum out of the rock there for about thirty years before it played out, which was about six years back. By that time, they had pretty well amortized the cost of the buildings, the mining gear and the transports."

Chameleon caught it before Juete: "You mean there are bloody transports just parked around *waiting* for us?"

Scanner shrugged. "No guarantees that anything there will run. But according to the records of the company working the area, all the heavy ground vehicles were cheaper to leave than to airlift out. No aircars, probably, but plenty of rolling stock."

"What about scavengers?" Sandoz asked. Again Scanner shook his head. "Like I said, no way to tell. It could be that everything was stripped. Six years is a long time, and with this climate, there might not be anything there but big piles of corrosion."

"You're risking our asses on a lot of maybes," Sandoz said to Dain.

Dain returned the gaze levelly. "I'm open to suggestions. If you've got a better idea, let's hear it."

Sandoz glared at him. Juete felt the assassin's rage boil briefly. She tensed—

Then Sandoz laughed. "No, I guess you're right, Maro. Skinny odds are better than none."

Dain stood up. "Let's get moving, then. I wouldn't be surprised if the warden sent somebody to check the back trail, just in case. The further away we get, the better."

Maro took the lead, wielding the machete. The thing's usefulness was almost done; whatever edge it had was gone, and the metal was bent and nicked. An hour later, he hit a particularly thick branch blocking their path, and the blade snapped in half. He stuck the remaining piece in his belt—it had a jagged point that might be useful for prying or stabbing—and they continued as best they could through the underbrush.

Around noon, Scanner took a sighting with the laser-compass. "Another ten klicks and we'll be out of this morass."

"Yeah? What then?" Chameleon asked.

"A stretch of the Teenig Desert extends a sandy finger up next to the swamp. Ecologically, it's a nightmare, but the sands have been creeping this way for a long time. Another hundred years, and this spot will probably be a dune. Forty klicks past that is the Girdle."

"Only forty kilometers. Why don't we do it backwards, just to make it interesting?"

Nobody acknowledged Chameleon's sarcasm. Maro was tired, and he knew the others were also. A forty-kilometer walk across a desert was not something to look forward to. The choices were limited at this point, however—it was that or go back to the Cage.

He looked at Juete and smiled. It would be worse on her than the others, even with the sunblock. He would have to try to figure out a way to cover her.

He stiffened suddenly. At the edge of his sight he caught Sandoz staring at Juete. Maro knew the look well enough. The man wanted her. Fortunately, he had better control of himself than most. Maro didn't want to think about what would happen if Sandoz lost that control. He could probably kill all of them without working up a major sweat. Worse, he still had the flare pistol, their only weapon. Maro hadn't asked for it back, and Sandoz hadn't offered it.

They moved, shoving aside the thick brush, wrapped in the heat and stink of the swamp. Right now, the desert would seem almost a relief.

Right now . . .

* nineteen *

"Report," Stark said. He leaned forward in his chair.

The voice from the holoproj image sounded hot and tired. "Nothing, Warden," the leader of the search said. "We've spread-and-pinched for a hundred klicks from the flitter. No sign of 'em."

Stark stared at the man's image, thinking quickly. "Could they have gotten some other form of transport onto the flitter with them? A cycle, or maybe another one of those jury-rigged repellor plates?"

"None of the cycles are missing, sir. It's possible they might have been able to stack a plate, but I don't think so. They couldn't have known they'd have mechanical failure."

He was right, Stark knew. "All right, then you've missed them. They didn't take a direct path to the port. Maybe they didn't know the right way to go."

"The flitter's laser-compass was missing—"

"Or maybe they went in another direction to throw us off. Sweep the main track again, then fan out from the flitter. Maybe they planned to move at angles before cutting back."

"Yessir. Discom."

Stark felt a flutter in his belly, a roiling like some small creature having a nightmare. It had been almost two full days since the escape, and his men should have found them by now. So far, he'd managed to keep the break confined to his own people, but within a few days Karnaaj was going to come storming in here, regulations or not, and then there would be the devil to pay. What could he do? They hadn't found any bodies, and Stark was certain that the escapees were still alive.

He would find them. He *had* to find them.

In the late afternoon they came to the end of the swamp. The mire didn't thin out—it simply stopped. They could see the edge of it a few hundred meters ahead, almost knife-sharp. Dead trees stuck up through sand drifts, some of which were twenty meters high. The swamp had swallowed what it could of the desert, but in the end, Juete thought, it had choked.

''Let's rest here for a while,'' Dain said. ''Sleep if we can. It makes a lot more sense to try the desert at night.''

Juete collapsed gratefully, leaning back against the rough bark of a tree. Sleep? She could sleep for a week!

''A night crossing might not be a good idea,'' Sandoz said. ''The sand will cool, and we'll stand out like bugs under a scope if they come looking for us.''

Scanner shook his head. ''There are hot spots; rocks buried under the sand, and like that. They'll have to check them all if they bother looking in this direction. During the day they can see us, but at night all they'll have are doppler and heatscopes. Better odds.''

Dain said, ''Besides, we only have three bottles of water. With the sun baking us, we won't be able to make forty klicks. If we push, we can cover twenty-five or thirty tonight, maybe more. Come morning, we can do the rest of it before it gets too hot.''

Chameleon asked, ''You really think we can walk that fast in sand?''

Dain looked at the metamorph. "We can try."

"What about animals?" That from Raze, who was brushing scum back from a small pond; after a moment, she began to dip and fill the water bottles. The bottles gurgled and bubbled in the green pool.

"No way to tell," Dain said.

"At least we can see them coming," Sandoz added.

"That won't do us much good if what's coming is a dragonbat."

Juete shifted against the tree, looking for a softer spot. There wasn't one. She felt her nerves begin to unknot ever so slightly. Two hours ago, something large had rattled the bushes not five meters away from them. Sandoz had snapped that flare pistol out so fast she wasn't sure she'd seen him move, and fired two shots. Whatever it was didn't like that much, for it crashed away from them, making a lot of noise in the process. It hadn't come back.

Raze dropped several of the water purification fizzies into the now-filled bottles. The liquid hissed. Juete did not care for the sterilized water—it had a strong chemical odor and tasted like chlorine—but it was better than risking whatever microscopic denizens normally inhabited it.

Dain turned away to look at the distant walls of sand. When he did, Juete felt Sandoz shift toward her. He dropped one hand and gently dragged his fingers along the side of her neck. Juete looked up, and Sandoz smiled at her. She dropped her gaze and saw that the front of his coverall bulged slightly at the crotch.

Trouble brewing.

He moved his hand away, deliberately but not hurriedly, as Dain turned back to face the others. There was no way that Dain could have missed Sandoz's touching her. He didn't say anything about it, though. Instead, he said, "We've got a few hours before it gets dark. We should take turns on watch while everybody else sleeps."

"Sounds good," Sandoz said. His voice had a sexual edge to it, something Juete recognized from long experience. "I'll take the first watch."

"Fine. Half an hour, then wake Chameleon. Give him the flare gun."

Sandoz's grin was lazy. "Sure."

To Chameleon, Dain said, "You wake Raze; Juete spells her, and I'll take the last one, if that's okay."

Nobody seemed to care. They spread the blankets out and everybody but Sandoz found a place. Juete curled up between Raze and Dain, and in a few minutes, despite this new situation to worry about, was asleep.

She had a dream. In it, she lay naked under Sandoz. Behind him Dain stood, fists clenched, but unable to move—his feet were covered with squirming vines that reached halfway up to his knees—as Sandoz pumped away in violent, driving strokes. She couldn't move either. Sandoz's pelvis pinned her hips, and Stark held one of her hands pressed to the swampy ground, while Berque held the other one. In the background, she heard the squealing of the myriad killer denizens of Omega, and the flutter of a million wings.

The horror of it was not what they were doing.

The horror of it was that she *enjoyed* it.

Maro watched through slitted lids the transfer of the flare gun from Sandoz to Chameleon. Sandoz knew what Maro was up to, that was all to obvious from the grin he had flashed earlier. *Why did I offer to take the last watch? Why, so I would wind up with the flare pistol when we started moving again*. Not that it mattered all that much; Sandoz was a lot deadlier without the weapon than Maro was with it. Still, there was no point in shading the odds in Sandoz's favor. A 12mm actinic-thermal flare in the eyes might swing things his way, if it came to that. And it might, it just might. Sandoz was used to being in control, inside the Cage and out. Juete was a spur, but not the only thing driving the assassin. Sooner or later he would feel compelled to take over. It was Maro's hope that it wouldn't happen until they reached the port, but that might be too much to wish for.

He finally dozed, but the sleep was not deep enough for dreams or real rest. It was bad enough that they had the warden and his guards and a killer planet to contend with; now, they had to worry about each other as well.

So much for honor among thieves.

Stark stood on the wall next to the south tower and the main gate. The sun was going down behind the opposite wall of the prison, giving view to another of the bright evening skies that on a civilized world would have been called beautiful. The rain had stopped, and it had come late enough to cool the air without turning to heavy vapor.

He looked to the south, past the M&T compound from which the prisoners had stolen the flitter. They were all going to die for this, he told himself. Except Juete. And she would pay dearly. Before he was done, she would kiss the ground he walked upon, and be happy for the privilege.

The intercom bell chimed softly from the tower. Stark did not turn. After a moment, the tower guard coughed behind him.

"Yes?"

"That was Reader in Communications, Warden. They've got the main transceiver repaired."

"Tell him to continue com silence."

". . . Yessir."

Stark turned back to stare over the Zonn construct into the jungle. He hated this world, he hated this goddamned job, and he hated Karnaaj. But more than all of it, he hated the prisoners who had escaped. He could cover it, if he caught them. No, not "if." *When* he caught them. But that nagging voice in his head kept asking the question he did not want to hear: What if you *don't* catch them? What will the Confed do to the man who let somebody escape from the Cage? Even if they die out there, unless you can prove it, you are as doomed as they are. What then, Officer Commander Warden?

What then?

"Dain?"

Maro sat up suddenly, disoriented. Juete kneeled nearby, one hand extended to touch him on the shoulder. He looked around. Dusk was fading into night, though it was still light enough to see clearly. The stink of decay seemed less; maybe it was the presence of all that clean, hot sand so close by. Scanner, Chameleon, Raze and Sandoz all appeared to be sleeping.

Maro moved carefully to avoid waking the others. He and Juete walked ten meters away, at which point she handed him the flare pistol.

"Are we going soon?" she asked.

"Another hour or so."

She glanced at the others, then back at Maro. "I don't think I can get back to sleep. Can I stay here with you?"

"Sure."

He was very aware of her sitting next to him, felt her call to him on a basic, primal level. Chemical, he knew, but also something more. He put one arm around her shoulders, and she pressed against him as though she had been doing it all her life. The contact felt comfortable, and more relaxed in that moment than it had with any woman he'd ever before been with.

"Dain?"

"Hmm?"

"There's a clear spot over there, behind those bushes."

He felt the heat rising from within, hotter than the damp air around them. "Yes."

They stood and moved out of sight of the others.

She kissed him, and Maro knew then that he had never felt this kind of power with any other lover. Her mouth was like fire on his, her tongue changing from soft to hard and back as she clutched at his back. He opened her coverall, bent and kissed her bright pink nipple. It hardened under his tongue. She moaned softly.

Lying on their clothes, sticky with humidity and sweat, they made love, touching, stroking, kissing, kneading each other's bodies. She was beautiful, as he had known she would be. Her pubic hair was snowy and soft, and when he kissed her mons, she tasted like salty honey. She came twice in that many minutes as he sucked and nibbled on her.

He managed to last all of three strokes the first time. He entered her, felt that incredible heat and tightness around him, and could not hold back.

The second time for him took longer and was even more intense. When he climaxed, he heard her whisper, "I love you!" and he could only nod, not trusting his voice.

Later, they sat up, slapping at the insects that had found bare patches in the repellent. They laughed softly together, smiling as they looked at each other.

"We'd better get dressed and wake them up," he finally said.

"I know. I love you. Thank you."

He laughed quietly. "Thank me? You got it wrong, lady. I'm the one who's grateful."

"Even trade, then?"

"No way. I got the best of the deal. Come on."

They stood and dressed, and went back to where the others slept. The night had claimed the tropics, and the stars and two of the three moons were peering out, casting their cold light into the darkness. Despite everything, despite all the danger and risk and exhaustion, Maro had never felt better in his life. Somehow, they might just make it. And if not, at least he had made a connection unlike any he had ever made before.

That was worth the trip in itself.

* twenty *

Compared to slogging through the swamp, the sand wasn't so bad. It was so different as to be almost pleasurable initially, walking and sinking in dryness. The sand got drier the further they got from the swamp, and for a while Juete liked the sound their feet made, almost a musical noise as the billions of tiny sand fragments rubbed against each other and the feet of the walkers.

It tired a whole new set of muscles, though. After an hour or so, her calves were cramping. Scanner took sightings with the laser-compass every few minutes, because they were walking around the tallest dunes and getting off their course. The last of the three moons was up, and it was easy enough to see in the washed out light.

It was an eerie trek. There was a little wind, making the air almost chilly. Aside from the occasional wraithlike plumes of sand that the breeze stirred, nothing moved on the desert except the six of them. There were short, clumpy plants now and then, fleshy-looking things about the size of a dinner plate that looked something like starfish. Then, two hours after they'd started, Sandoz, in the lead, suddenly said "Everybody down!"

They were just cresting a short rise. Juete dropped, as

did the others. Dain slithered up to where Sandoz lay. The others, including Juete, also centimetered their way toward the top of the dune.

Once there, she saw what Sandoz had spotted. A few dozen meters away was a beast. It looked vaguely like holos she had once seen of a horse, but it was stumpier, with thicker legs and a fat, smooth, black body. The ears were large, almost leaf-shaped, and its tail was a hairless cord that nearly touched the ground. The thing appeared to be eating something on the sand.

Sandoz whispered, "Scanner, you know what it is?"

"Never saw anything like it," Scanner replied.

"Dangerous, do you think?" Chameleon said.

Dain said, "Probably not. It looks like a herbivore. It's nibbling one of those succulent plants, see?"

Dain pointed at the ground, and Juete could see that what he said was true. Then, though no one had moved, something must have startled the creature, for it suddenly whipped its head up and stared directly at them. It didn't seem to see them, but the animal snorted as if testing the air for scents. Then, abruptly, it turned and trotted off. Juete saw that the animal's feet were very broad and flat, almost semicircular. They kept it from sinking into the sand very far, despite its bulk.

"I wonder if they're good to eat," Raze said. "Those rations we have don't stick too well. And they won't last past tomorrow, no matter how we slice 'em."

"How're you planning to nail it, Raze? Scare it to death?"

Raze grinned at Chameleon. "You're the one whose got a face that would fry a security circuit. Maybe that's not a bad idea."

"Come on," Dain said. "Best we get moving again."

Juete stood and shook the sand out of her coverall. She was abruptly aware of Sandoz watching her movements, and she stopped. Better to be a little sandy than to give him any reason to heat up.

After another hour, it became apparent that they weren't going to make as much speed as Dain had hoped they would. It was fine on the flat stretches, where the sand was packed fairly tight, but on the slopes of the dunes it was two steps up and one step back. They sank to their knees, and Juete's lower legs were scraped and raw before they had walked ten kilometers. On the downside of the dunes, they could let gravity do a lot of the work, but they often fell, and rolling in sand was not enjoyable after walking in it for several hours.

They came to a sort of pass that meandered through several large dunes. The footing seemed almost solid, and Juete was grateful for small favors as she trudged along with the others. Scanner had taken the lead, followed by Raze and Dain, with Chameleon and Sandoz bringing up the rear behind Juete. It was by far the easiest walking they had done. If it stayed this way for a few more kilometers, they would be across the desert in another couple of hours . . .

Then, under the moonlight, Scanner yelled suddenly. Juete was looking right at him when he sank, disappearing into the sand like a man stepping onto the surface of a lake. Only one arm and hand remained in sight, and that was sinking rapidly.

As she watched, immobilized by shock and surprise, Scanner's hand vanished beneath the sand.

Stark stood under the lights outside of his personal storage shed, a prefab stress plastic block nestled behind the fence in the northeast corner of the Stores yard. Thousands of insects buzzed the lights above. Weird shadows danced over him as the insects fitfully bounced against the glass of the HT lamps. The shed was locked, and would open only to the palm signature of his right hand. The warden stared at the translucent green building as if he could see through it to what was inside.

Don't panic, he told himself. *It's not time yet.*

"Warden Stark?" came the voice from his com.

"Yes?"

"The search team leader is reporting in."

"Put it through."

"Copy. Stand by."

The team leader came on. "We've lasered half a dozen big animals in the swamp, but there's no sign of the prisoners, either visual or on sensors."

"What about the back trails? Any signs?"

"Ah, that's negative. Simmons says he's seen sand deer and a lot of dry ground, but no tracks. He's gotten some subsurface readings, but they've all turned out to be rocks or outcrops."

"Keep looking. They're out there."

"Unless they sank in the swamp or something ate them."

"Say again, search leader." His voice was cold and even.

He heard the man swallow. "Sorry, Warden. Search pattern continuing."

"Copy. Discom."

He walked to the stress plastic building and put one hand onto the surface. Warm, even this late at night. He turned away. He was tired. He needed to rest. The bastards were making him react, he was not in control, and he did not like it.

There was really no reason to worry. After all, he had the information from Maro, via Berque, to fall back upon.

Oh? said the malevolent little voice inside his head. *Really? As slick as the escape went, and Berque going with them; do you really think what Berque told you is true? You know Maro was behind this escape, don't you? Remember how he withstood the Zonn Chamber? You don't have anything for back-up here, Stark old buddy, not a goddamn thing, so let's not fool ourselves, hey? Go and take a nap, but don't stop worrying, because you've got* plenty *to worry about.*

Stark moved away from the small building toward the gate in the fence around Stores. Sleep, if he could manage it, that would help. He'd be better after a few hours of sleep.

He hoped . . .

Raze yelled "Chain up! Grab my arm!" at Maro. He reached out and caught her wrist, feeling her lock onto his at the same moment with powerful fingers. He extended his other arm, and Juete grabbed it with both hands. He spared her a glance in time to see Chameleon clutch Juete around the waist in a tight hug. Sandoz was moving toward Chameleon, and Maro turned back toward Raze, who dropped to her knees, pulling Maro with her. The others went down, dominolike, as Raze jammed her free hand down into the sand, stirring the powdery substance as she groped for Scanner.

It seemed like a long time, but it could only have been a few seconds before she yelled again. "Got him!" Maro's shoulder felt like it was being torn loose as Raze contracted the muscles of her upper body. Scanner's hand cleared the sand, followed by his arm and then his head. He coughed violently as Raze, anchored by Maro and the others, dragged him free of the sand. His shoulders and chest appeared, then his hips. He pawed at the sand with his free hand as if swimming, and after a moment his feet came out of the treacherous ground.

"Back up!" Maro commanded.

The chain of people shuffled backward, dragging the still-coughing Scanner. In another moment they were clear of the trap.

Chameleon laughed, a release of tension, and Maro felt the urge to join him. That had been close—

The ground started to vibrate. Two meters behind Scanner, the sand began to churn. It erupted upward suddenly into a cloud of fine particles and a rattle of . . . bones.

Maro saw clearly the dead, dry bones as they showered down, long ones, ribs, an oblong skull, thumping and sinking back out of sight into the sand.

Then, out of the sand came a nightmare.

It looked vaguely spiderlike, in that it had a lot of legs, but it seemed to be as big as Maro's cell. The limbs were short and paddle-shaped, and centered in the top of the fat, brown oblong body was a gaping hole surrounded by three or four sets of serrated pincers. *That would be the mouth,* Maro thought, almost calmly. The thing didn't seem to have any eyes, but then, it didn't seem to need any.

The sand monster scrabbled easily toward Scanner, its body tilted, hind legs rearing it up so that the mouth was almost parallel to the ground. Maro released Raze's wrist and grabbed for the flare pistol. He dropped it, snatched it up, and managed to get to his knees. The rest of it was almost instinctive. He pointed the weapon at the monster's open mouth and fired as fast as he could pull the trigger. The gun spat four flares. Three of them went into the thing's maw before it could close the opening; the fourth flare hit the armored carapace as the mouth snapped shut, bounced high into the air trailing red, and landed twenty meters away to sizzle on the desert floor.

The monster opened its mouth again and screamed. Smoke poured out with the sound, and the light of the burning flares looked even redder than usual. The thing shook its body back and forth, then backed away. Maro caught the odor of burning tissue, a nidorous smell, as the thing roared again, its cry like that of a woman screaming in pain.

Without realizing his actions, Maro reloaded the flare pistol, then held it extended with both hands, aimed at the monster. It wasn't necessary. The thing's legs churned the surface, flippers showering Scanner and Raze with buckets of the fine, dustlike sand as the creature swiftly dug its way back out of sight. The ground rumbled for a moment, then faded to stillness.

Maro stood, flare gun still pointed at the now-quiet patch of almost liquid sand. The others got to their feet. The silence was unbroken until Chameleon said, "What the fuck was *that*?"

"I don't know," Maro said. "But I don't want to be anywhere near here if it comes back."

"Amen," Raze said.

Maro looked at her, then the others. "As long as we're on this kind of flat stretch, we hold hands. Anybody object to that?"

Nobody did. "I'll take the lead," Maro continued. "If I hit one of these traps, try and pull me out. If you can't, let go and run like hell."

From the looks on their faces, it didn't seem as if he would need to worry much about that.

Juete's energy was just about gone. She walked mechanically, glad to have Raze's hand on the one side and Scanner's on the other. They weren't walking single file any more, but at about a forty degree angle, with Dain leading. Any of them could step into another pit, but as bunched up as they were, it was likely Dain would hit it first.

"I don't think we'll run into another of those things for a while," Scanner said.

"What makes you think so?" Juete asked.

"I don't think the desert will support too many of them. They eat those horse-things, looks like, and we haven't seen a lot of them. Something that big must eat a fair amount, and if there were too many of them around, they'd starve."

Sandoz said, "That sounds pretty good, but what if the thing has more than one trap? I'd think it had a bunch—otherwise, it might be a long time before it caught anything."

"I think maybe this one won't be interested in checking

his traps for a little while,'' Raze put in. ''Too much pepper in its last meal.''

Dain laughed at that, and the sound made Juete's pulse speed up. She liked hearing him laugh.

Both Scanner and Raze squeezed her hands then, almost at the same instant. They had felt her joy, her excitement. She felt as if she could trust Scanner and Raze, at least for now, and she returned the hand pressure. She had learned the hard way that you had to take your friends where you could find them. And friends were something to look for, especially when you were as vulnerable as were the albinos of Rim.

The moons began to set, and the sky gradually grew darker, even under the luminous swath of stars that swept across the heavens. The six escapees walked across the sea of sand, still alive for now. That was something, at least. They weren't dead yet, and that was in itself a kind of miracle.

But they hadn't really escaped yet, either. If Dain and Scanner's mining site was there, if they could get a vehicle working and if the warden's guards didn't find them, then they had a chance. It was a lot of ''ifs,'' she knew, and any one of them could short the whole plan. And another whole set of questions lay beyond these: could they get a ship and get offworld? That was the only way they would stay alive, and that was the biggest worry of all.

Juete mentally shrugged. One miracle at a time.

✳ twenty-one ✳

Stark awoke just before dawn, after no more than two or three hours of sleep. He lay on the bed for a few minutes, but knew he wasn't going to recapture that blessed unconsciousness. He got up, showered and dressed, and went to his office.

He felt a little better than he had; some sleep was better than none. He powered up his desk terminal. Time to review his options.

There were things he could do to catch the prisoners. He could call Omega City for help. They would footprint the likely routes of the escapees with one of their looksats, and probably pick up the bastards within a pass or two. That would solve one problem, but it wouldn't do him any good personally. Getting them back wasn't as important as keeping quiet the fact that they were out in the first place. He knew there was no way he could keep a lid on it forever; eventually, it would get out. But if he caught them before it happened, then it would not be a real escape. The Confed might grumble, but I-took-care-of-it-myself was a prime defense for any kind of military snafu.

He could keep his men searching for another day or two in hopes of nailing the runners. He could expect that much time before Karnaaj really started throwing his weight around. By then, he could smile and blandly assure the SDI ghoul that there had been some trouble, but it was all in the past, and here's Maro for you. Juete? Oh, she had an accident. Dead, I'm afraid. Cremated, of course. Pity, but there it is. Fortunes of war, what?

As a last resort, there was the Juggernaut—that option was becoming more attractive all the time. He still might be able to use it and keep it quiet long enough to dump it where it would never be found.

Or he could always simply open a line to Confed HQ for the sector, tell them he had an escape, and throw himself upon their mercy. Which would be rather like throwing himself upon a thicket of poisoned spikes.

None of the solutions seemed very appealing, but it wasn't time to panic yet. In two more days he would make the hard decisions. Until then, he would keep things as they were.

Maro could understand why desert cultures had so many different words to describe sand; otherwise, every sentence about the terrain would be so adjective-laden as to collapse under its own weight. There was the hard-packed sand of the flat sections, ridged by the wind into waterlike ripples; powdery drifts like dry snow; cakelike crusts atop ridges that left gaping holes under each footstep, and half a dozen other variations, none of which seemed very much like any of the others.

At this point, as the sun began to lighten the sky, Maro had seen enough of different kinds of sand to last him a lifetime.

"We should be getting close," Scanner said.

Maro nodded. "Good. Why don't we take a break here, and I'll climb that dune and see what I can see."

The dune loomed just ahead, rising a good thirty meters above the desert floor. Nobody argued, and nobody volunteered to go along. Maro gave a tight grin that hurt his dried skin. They were tired, as was he, but nobody was complaining, either.

A wind was rising, swirling the more powdery sand around like dust. The others walked to the base of the dune where the wind was less, and collapsed on the cool and soft drift. Maro circled toward the end of the dune; experience had taught them that trying to climb up the drifted sides took too much energy. Sinking hip-deep made for slow movement. Where the dune tapered down, the crustier cap material allowed for somewhat better footing if one moved slowly and carefully.

It took about fifteen minutes of step-crunch, step-crunch, to reach the peak. The breeze was harder here, tugging at his clothes, and the fine sand formed a stone wind that abraded and stung where it touched bare skin.

Scanner had been right. To the east, the seemingly endless drifts and dunes came to an abrupt end. There were trees and rocks there, perhaps five kilometers away. Just beyond that, Maro thought he could see the line of rocks known as the Girdle. Somewhere on that hard strip was their destination.

He turned and looked down at the others. They were below and to his left. Going down would be easier; gravity could do the work, and it didn't matter if he sank somewhat. He started to step off the harder surface of the dune for the descent when he heard the sound.

In the distance, there came the whine of a small engine.

Maro searched the skies. The sunlight was not up to full strength, but he made out a dot skimming well above the tallest dunes, moving toward him. It was hard to say for sure, but it looked like a single-person cycle.

In another minute it would be right on top of them.

Stark moved as if an amphetaminic coursed through his system, flogging each nerve, whispering insistently for action, movement, speed! He walked the wall, the Zonn metal slick beneath his boots, and stared off into the distance. It was almost as if he might somehow *will* the escapees to return by being there, act like some sort of biological magnet, drawing them to himself.

Foolish thought, of course. He knew he should remain calm, should wait for his people to locate their quarry, should avoid doing anything rash. But those thoughts came from the mind, borne of his intellect; his gut, which churned up emotions much more primal, called for him to *do* something, and do it now!

It had always been so with him, and he wondered at times if other people had the same war ongoing inside. The age-old battle between the neocortex, secure in its military background, counselling caution, procedure and patience; and, opposing, the hindbrain, the reptilian remnant, shouting without subtlety about fight-or-flight and self-preservation.

Usually, the intellect won out; usually, but not always. Sometimes jungle reaction *was* the proper response; sometimes doing something, *anything*, turned out to be better than doing nothing. And there was no way to know, of course, when a man should turn loose the hormonal hounds and let them run and bay. Therein lay the problem. More and more, he was feeling that it was time to move, to put himself into the field, even though he was not sure of the wisdom of it.

Stark stared at the cleared patch between the wall and the bush. Something darted out of the trees, a lizardlike creature. It thought better of its action, turned and ran back to cover.

He understood exactly what the thing must have felt.

A sign. He needed a sign of some kind. Before, he had always gotten some form of indicator, a pointer that made the decision more justifiable, whether yea or nay. It might only be a rationalization, but when it happened, he knew it for what it was.

So. Give it another day or two. If nothing happened, he would know that he was doing the right thing. If the cosmic finger touched him, however, that would be something else again.

And more and more, he was beginning to hope for that sign . . .

Juete heard Dain yelling, but at first the sound was so garbled by the wind that she couldn't understand what he was trying to say. Then, next to her, Scanner said "Oh, *shit!*" about the same time that she caught part of what Dain was saying.

"—aircycle! Dig in! Get out of sight!"

Raze was already stripping off her shirt and wrapping it around her head. Her flat breasts rippled with muscle as she turned and began to burrow into the base of the dune.

"Get flat!" Scanner ordered. "Cover your nose and mouth, breath slow and evenly! Stay down until he passes!"

Juete felt the still-cool sand cascade over her as Scanner shoveled with his hands, burying her. Even under the cupped bowl of her hands the sand trickled into her face, and she sneezed. Around her she could feel the sand vibrating as the others covered themselves. After a moment, things got still.

She kept her eyes squeezed tightly closed, and the sand pressed against her ears. It was hard to breathe, but the layer over her head was shallow, and her hands kept enough of a pocket for some air. Not enough for long, she realized. Not enough air would filter through the sand, whether shallow or not.

She was not afraid. Being alone had frightened her to the point of mindless terror, but claustrophobia had never been one of her fears. The others were all around her; she could feel somebody's leg twitching slightly near her left foot. It was oddly comforting.

She heard the approach of the aircycle. The drone was

muted, but loud enough to penetrate her cover. The thing passed overhead, off to one side. Good! But then the fading drone returned. He must be circling back. It grew louder. She felt it through the sand—strange that sand would carry vibrations so well—and then there was an abrupt cut off to it.

It was getting harder to breathe. The air she had trapped was hot and growing foul. She was trying to sip at it, taking small and even breaths, but the urge to sit up and inhale deeply was growing. It couldn't have been more than a minute since Scanner had covered her, but it felt like a lot longer.

Somebody walked toward her. She felt the steps. They seemed impossibly loud, as if a giant were slogging across the desert, about to step on her. Then they stopped, very near. What was he doing? Not that it mattered; in another ten or fifteen seconds, she was going to have to have air, no matter who was out there, even if it were Stark himself. There was no way to get around it. Her lungs were crying for oxygen now, and if something didn't happen soon—

Somebody screamed, a primal, guttural yell, the call of a killing predator about to take prey.

Juete sat up. The thin layer of sand oozed away from her. She shook her head to clear her ears, and opened her eyes at the same instant.

A guard stood not two meters away, a heavy pulse pistol in his hands. His attention was elsewhere, however; he was staring upward, a look of astonishment on his face, his body frozen. She saw him flick a glance in her direction, but immediately he jerked his gaze back toward the dune.

Juete twisted to see what the guard saw. Dain bounded down the side of the dune, screaming and waving his arms. Sand showered from his steps, but he was ten meters away and moving slowly for all his efforts and noise. *He must have buried himself under the dune,* she thought.

The guard's momentary paralysis wore off; he whipped the pulse pistol up and fired. His aim was off. Juete heard the hard thrum of the weapon, saw the sand splash and glassify under the bolt a meter to Dain's left. Dain kept coming. The guard corrected his aim, prepared to fire again—

And all around her, the sand erupted. The guard started, surprised by this new threat. He swung the gun around.

Chameleon was closer, but Sandoz got there first. He slammed one elbow into the guard's temple. Before the man could fall, the assassin struck again, the fingers of the same hand and arm extended into an open-handed ridge that smashed the opposite temple. The man's head snapped to one side as if struck by a club, and he fell bonelessly to the sand. The pulse pistol flew from his hand and landed next to Juete. The tip of the barrel smoked as the sand touched it.

Dain slid the last meter down the face of the dune. He moved to the fallen guard. Raze had her hand on the man's neck, feeling for a pulse.

"Nobody home here anymore," she said, leaning back.

Chameleon laughed nervously. "Nice work," he said to Sandoz.

"Thanks," Sandoz replied, almost absently.

"Troubles," Scanner said. "If he called for back-up—"

"He didn't have time to com anything," Chameleon said. Then, uncertainly, "You think?"

"Probably not," Dain said. "But even if he doesn't call in, they'll come looking for him."

"Great," Sandoz said. "Fucking great. If I had just gone for the stun we'd have a prisoner who could've sent them off to the goddamned moons looking for us!" He smacked the heel of his hand against his temple. "Stupid!"

"Well," Raze said, "at least we've got a weapon and a cycle. Maybe we can do some damage before they take us."

"No, wait," Juete found herself saying. "There's a better way."

The others turned to look at her. Dain said, "You have an idea?"

She stood and shook sand out of her hair. "What if he had an accident? If they found him then, they wouldn't connect him to us, would they?"

Scanner and Dain exchanged glances. Scanner said, "He's probably been looking at rocks all over the desert all night. Heat-scan gear on the cycle. I doubt he would have called in each time he landed to dig up a hot boulder."

"So?" That from Chameleon.

Dain looked thoughtful. "So, Juete's right. If something happened to his cycle—maybe he got sand in one of the repellors, like that—and he crashed and fractured his skull, it would be an accident. They'd come looking for him, but they wouldn't be looking for us."

Scanner said. "They don't have vox ID at the prison. I could fuzz the com on the cycle, send in a garbled message, something like, 'My cycle's acting up, I'm gonna try to nurse it back to the flitter.' "

Dain smiled. "You're a genius, you know that?"

"I've always thought so, myself."

"Maybe we could even have this guy—" Raze nodded at the corpse, "—tell them he'd checked the whole desert and it was clear."

"Better not get too complicated," Scanner said. "We don't know how long he's been out here or what he's said before."

"Right," Dain said. "Let's keep it simple."

Maro watched as Raze and Sandoz loaded the body onto the aircycle. The machine bobbed as it adjusted to the weight. Raze arranged the corpse so that it would stay on, draping it between the protective side rails used for carrying cargo. The message had gone like Scanner had planned. He had used the tool kit under the cycle's seat to make a break in the com circuit. Even if they checked, he said, they'd never notice that it was done on purpose.

"Ready," Raze said.

Sandoz pulled the pulse pistol from his belt and gazed at it fondly before shoving it into the guard's holster. That had been a sore point with him, but if they had kept it, that would surely have raised suspicions. It was unlikely that the guards would believe it had vanished on impact, and even so, a routine sweep with a detector would turn it up if that were the case. Better to let it go with the guard.

Scanner twisted the throttle and gunned the engine. He had rigged it to stay on until the cycle reached the end of its journey—a trip that should last about two kilometers, they figured. At this height, the ground was more or less flat for that far before a series of dunes crossed the flight path. The cycle would plow into one of those at speed, a collision that would surely have killed the man were he not already dead.

"Give my regards to the devil," Sandoz said as he thumbed the aircycle into forward gear. The machine sped off, arrow straight, flying at chest height.

They watched it for a moment before Maro said, "Come on, let's go. We won't be able to see it hit."

The cycle had given them another tool they had not figured on. They couldn't take anything physical, but Scanner had figured out the lock frequency the guards were using for their operation. Without the codes, a com would only receive garbled static; with them, the transceiver they had taken from the downed flitter was now able to receive and decipher the opchan. Maybe they might get enough warning to hide if somebody else came their way.

Almost out of the desert, Maro thought. Another hour and they would be back in the safety of cover. It could be a lot worse.

They still had a chance.

✳ twenty-two ✳

Alarms blared, and Stark's office com lit with incoming warnings from his guards: there was a force of Confederation Military cruising toward the prison, bleeding all over the operational channels and demanding to speak to the warden. Stark nodded grimly to himself. Karnaaj of the *Soldatutmarkt* had arrived, bearing not gifts, but guns.

Well, Stark, said the smirking voice inside his head, *if ever you needed a sign, here it is.*

Stark sighed and, almost as if he were viewing the movements of some other poor, doomed soul, watched his hand reach for the com.

"Commander Stark." Karnaaj's voice was as cold as he remembered it. "I think you have some explaining to do."

Might as well attack, Stark thought. *What the hell.* "Perhaps, Commander Karnaaj, but maybe first *you'd* better explain why you countermanded my authority on radio silence and Military Emergency Priority Status—"

"Let's not play games here, Stark. I wouldn't be here if I didn't have the clout."

True, Stark thought, *and we both know it.* But he had to go through the motions. "All right, Commander. I have a situation here that—"

"State the nature of it," Karnaaj demanded. His voice was like a coiled steel snake, tightly wound and set to strike.

Stark closed his eyes. "An escape. Seven prisoners."

He was glad he couldn't see Karnaaj's face on the restricted channel. There was an ominous moment of silence—then: "You declared a Priority Emergency for an *escape*? For *seven* prisoners?" Karnaaj's tone promised retribution for this that would pale the face of a medieval inquisitor.

Time to drop the bomb. "One of them was Maro, Commander. Recall how valuable you told me he was?"

There was another moment of silence after that—but it felt different. Stark had a sudden gut reaction. Something was wrong with Karnaaj's interest in Maro; there was more going on here than showed on the surface. The SDI officer wasn't simply carrying out Confed policy. With the instinct of a good warrior seeing a chink in the enemy's armor, Stark struck. "I wanted to handle the matter myself, which is why I haven't put out a planetwide alert or called in the recon satellites yet. But if you like, I can do that now—"

"No! I mean, I—ah—see the wisdom of your decision, Warden Stark. It would be easier if we handled this ourselves. No point in bringing in any more people."

Stark grinned fiercely. So the unflappable Karnaaj *didn't* want the Confed looking over his shoulder on this. Interesting. Very interesting. For the moment, then, they were on the same side. It might be a rogues' alliance, but it was better than none. Karnaaj had a weak spot, and Stark had just found part of it.

He might just come out of this alive . . .

Maro thought that the straggly trees and underbrush that appeared when the sands faded into harder earth were the most beautiful things he had ever seen. When the canopy closed in overhead and the ground growth thinned he felt immeasurably safer than he had on the desert.

Occasionally, the small transceiver that he now carried would crackle with talk on the search opchan, but from the sound of it, the guards were still fanned out in the opposite direction.

Another hour's walk brought them to the Girdle; thirty minutes after that they were at the mining site.

It was amazing. The jagged scar of the strip-mining operation had been smoothed but little by the few years of weather, but the area was littered with rusty machinery. How could they have simply *left* all this? There were worlds in the galaxy where just the metal of the abandoned gear would be worth a fortune, not to mention the motors and engines contained therein. Some of the devices for moving rock were ten meters tall and twice that length, with treads the height of a tall man; and everywhere, it seemed, smaller machines sat where they had been left, as though waiting for their operators to return and continue working.

"Let's do a quick survey and see what all we've got here," the smuggler said. Sandoz muttered something under his breath. Maro turned to him. "I didn't catch that."

"Nothing."

They split up into pairs. Scanner and Raze went to the north, Sandoz and Chameleon to the south, and Maro and Juete to the east, toward the edge of the Girdle itself.

An hour later the six met back at the Admin building, which was roughly in the center of the mining camp.

Scanner said, "Mostly housing to the north. The rec hall, cafeteria, like that. But we found Stores, and maybe half a dozen three-man carts. They're surface vehicles, with fat tires, but I think I can get them running."

Maro nodded. "Juete and I found Operations One. Most of the place had been cleared, but there are three GE shovel-loaders parked out back on the edge of the Girdle. Nothing else useful."

It was Sandoz's turn, and he looked like a man with a secret. "Me and the skin-shifter found Op Two, and it was pretty well cleaned out, too. There's something called a—what was it?"

"Sort Separator," Chameleon put it.

"Yeah, a Sort Separator, that looks in pretty good shape. I don't know what it does, but there's a lot of motors on it. And we found Maintenance. Somebody left a whole shitload of tools behind. Wrenches, welders, power sockets, like that. And a broadcast generator with two drums of fuel, too."

Scanner laughed in delight. "Tools and power! We can do it! I'd bet demi-stads to toenails that I can cobble a GE repellor to one of those carts and give us wings!"

"How long?" Maro asked.

"Two days, maybe less, if we all help. It won't be pretty and it won't be fast, but if we have any luck at all, we can make it work."

"We've been walking all night," Maro said. "We should get a few hours' sleep first. I'd hate to see anybody burn off a hand because he passed out."

Nobody argued with that.

Juete woke with a full bladder. Dain slept next to her, but he didn't move when she got up. They had chosen one of the small housing units just north of the Admin building. It had two sleeping rooms and a fresher unit. The others were in similar buildings in rows of a dozen such. She went to the fresher, but the chemical toilet had long since gone sour and died, so she moved outside, walked around behind the house, untabbed her coverall and squatted. She had gotten used to doing that the last few days.

As she stood and began to retab her coverall, Sandoz stepped around the corner in front of her.

Juete felt a cold finger of fear touch her spine. The assassin indicated the coverall. "Take it off."

"What?"

"You heard me." He reached for the tabs on his own coverall and began to pull them open. She didn't have to look; she could sense his erection.

She felt the familiar remoteness, the insulating emotional shutdown, begin. It was not important. He wanted to fuck her and it would be the simplest thing to let him. He could probably kill her without raising his heartbeat; worse, he could hurt Dain or the others. It would cost her maybe five minutes, and he didn't have the look of a man who enjoyed giving pain with his sex. It would hurt nobody. She had done worse.

The situation had been too good to last.

She started to strip.

"No," came Raze's voice.

Juete turned and saw the woman standing there. Sandoz turned also. "Stay out of this," he ordered.

"It's all right," Juete said to Raze.

Looked from her to Sandoz, then back to her. "Do you want this?" Raze asked her.

Juete shrugged. "It doesn't matter. He does, and it's not that important to me."

Raze took a step, shifting her left foot forward and turning slightly to the side. "Well, it's important to me," she said. "Rape is rape."

Sandoz hadn't bothered to retab his coverall, but he shifted his stance to mirror Raze's. "I can take you, you know that," he said softly.

"Probably. But I'll hurt you before you do."

"I've been hurt before."

Raze's voice was as soft as Sandoz's. "Listen to me. If we start this, it's all the way, understand? You'll have to kill me, and I'll do my damnedest to kill you. I might not succeed. But even if all I do is break your leg, where does that leave you? In the middle of hell with the demons looking for you."

Juete could see Sandoz thinking about that. It seemed like a long time passed. Weeks. Years. Eons.

Finally, as the universe approached heat death, Sandoz stepped back and straightened. "It's not worth having to kill you just to screw her," he said. "She wants it, she has to have it, and sooner or later, I'll be around when she comes into heat. I can wait."

Raze held her stance as Sandoz turned and strolled away. Then she relaxed and let out a long breath. "You okay?" she asked.

Juete also remembered how to breathe again. "Yes. Thank you."

"You don't have to let them have you. You don't have to do anything you don't want to. You're free, now."

Tears welled and spilled from Juete's eyes. If only that were true! How would it feel, to really be free? "Th-thank you, Raze." She stepped forward and hugged the other woman, feeling the hard muscle under her hands and against her own body.

Raze hugged her back for a moment, then caught her shoulders and gently pushed Juete away. There was something in the way she did it that made Juete ask, "Is anything wrong?"

"No. Nothing."

Not quite sure why, Juete hesitantly reached out and stroked Raze's cheek. "You're a good friend, Raze."

Raze caught her hand. "Look, I didn't save you from Sandoz just to play with you myself."

Juete blinked in surprise. "I didn't say you did."

Raze was obviously uncomfortable. She avoided the albino's gaze. "I'm not that way, you know. Everyone thinks so—everyone thinks that just because I've got muscles I've got to be a dyke."

Juete said nothing. After a moment, Raze gave a short, uncomfortable laugh and looked at her. "Sorry. I get tired of explaining, y'know?"

Gently, Juete asked, "Have you ever tried it?"

She thought she saw a momentary flash of fear in Raze's eyes. "No."

Juete felt a strong desire to touch this powerful woman, to kiss and stroke and be with her. "You trust me?"

Raze looked puzzled for a moment. "Yeah. Funny, isn't it?"

Juete raised herself slightly and kissed Raze. Her practiced mouth overcame Raze's initial resistance. She heard and felt Raze's breath grow ragged, and the small moan that escaped.

"I want you," Juete said.

"You sure?"

"Yes. And that's the difference between you and Sandoz. You care what I want."

They went back into the house. Raze stiffened when she saw Dain, still asleep on the bed.

"It's all right. He won't mind," Juete said.

"I dunno—"

Juete leaned over him. "Dain?"

He rolled over and blinked sleepily at the two women.

"Raze and I want to be together. We'll be in the next room. Is that okay?"

He smiled. "Sure. Have a good time." He rolled back over.

"Jesu," Raze said softly. "You'd better hang onto him. He's a keeper."

"I intend to. But for now, I want to hang onto you. Come on."

She took Raze's hand and led her into the next room.

Stark and Karnaaj faced each other over Stark's desk. For once the warden felt that he held, if not the upper, then at least an equal hand.

He had explained the procedure for locating the escapees. Karnaaj had merely nodded and ordered the two dozen troops he had brought into the field to help Stark's guards. While Stark did not trust Karnaaj's soldiers and was certain Karnaaj felt the same about his guards, he was sure that each of them could control his own troops.

So—rather than an enemy, Karnaaj was, for the moment at least, an ally. Stark would trust him no further than he could shot-put the planet he stood on, and he was certain that once Maro and the others were retrieved the alliance would be off; still, it was a better situation than before.

Except for Juete. He was not yet ready to bargain her away. He loved her, he knew that, and Karnaaj would only use her for a while before he grew bored and destroyed her. Stark did not want that to happen. Somehow he had to find Juete before Karnaaj did, and hide her from the man's grasp. He had some ideas as to how to do that, but they would have to wait until the escapees were located.

In the meantime, he would be polite. And cautious.

Maro dozed. He heard the sounds of the two women making love in the next room, and even caught the faint scent of sexual musk from them. It was exciting, but he felt no particular jealousy of Raze. Juete had told him what she was, and he understood it, or at least thought he did. It had been hard for her, this trek, and he didn't want to add to it. Besides, one could not possess another man or woman—he had learned that in his studies of the spirit. He loved Juete for what she was, not for what he would have her be, and her sexual drive was a large part of her.

Which was not to say that he would mind being in there with the two women, but he hadn't been invited.

Maybe next time, he thought, as he slipped completely back into slumber.

✱ twenty-three ✱

Scanner was like a child with a room full of new toys. Maro smiled as the circuit-rider babbled about the equipment he'd found.

"I can't believe they *left* this. Look! The circuits in this control box are worth six months' pay, easy! There's not a spot of corrosion on it! Christus, if I'd had this in the Cage, I could have run the whole place."

They were in the Maintenance building, where a rapidly growing pile of mechanical and electronic components lay spread out on work benches and the floor. Chameleon ran a power socket nearby, stripping nuts from a repellor assembly, while Raze and Juete pushed one of the carts into the work bay. Sandoz fiddled with a laser torch, and Maro dug through a spare-parts bin, trying to fill Scanner's list. There was the coil-and-arrestor assembly he needed . . .

Maro looked toward the work bays. The cart Juete and Raze moved into place stood next to another. They were boxy rectangles with the front end angled into a blunt point, the bodies made of stacked graphites, with a plastic windshield and no top. The operator sat in front, while two friendly passengers could squeeze into small seats behind him. The wheels were fat slunglas radials, two to a side.

The whole unit was maybe three meters long, and a trip of any distance wouldn't be the most comfortable ride anybody had ever taken. But it sure beat walking.

They would need two of them, unless they wanted to sit on top of each other. Scanner was confident that he could get the pair running, though he was having trouble with one of the scavenged repellor circuits.

"See, we can link the systems, here and here, and get a kind of ground effect. Probably can't balance it good enough to fly more than a meter off the ground, and it'd be better to run on the surface whenever possible. We'll need two sets of controls. I can recircuit the repellor to a slave, here." He pointed to a jury-rigged aluminum box. "But it'll be tricky to run. I can do it direct, through the computer, but manual will be a bitch."

Then he was off in technical land again, spouting electronic language as if it were his native tongue. Maro caught about every fifth word. He understood the gist of it, though. If it worked, they had transportation.

Red light flared behind him. Sandoz had the laser welder working. It was a small unit, about the size of a man's arm, not counting the power supply. That was strapped onto his back like a knapsack. The assassin adjusted the controls, and a bright needle a meter long stabbed out from the nozzle. Grinning, Sandoz waved the thing back and forth like a sword.

"Saw part of an old, old flatvid once," he said to no one in particular. "Back from the nineteenth or twentieth century. Had guys running around and fighting with things like this."

Maro turned back to his scavenging. The welder was a tool, but it would also serve just as well as a weapon. Maro was only too aware of that. He had been keeping his eyes open for something more powerful than the flare pistol; he had the feeling he would need it to stay ahead of Sandoz. In the assassin's hands, almost anything could be made deadly. Maro only had a few flares left for the pistol, and he wasn't sure of the damage he could do against a man in any event. Especially a man like Sandoz.

The transceiver crackled, and voices went back and forth over the operations channel. Everybody stopped to listen, save Scanner.

The talk centered on the search. After a few exchanges, however, it stopped. Maro let out a relieved breath. Earlier the channel had been alive with new voices. Stark had gotten some help, it seemed, and Commander Karnaaj's name was mentioned at one point. Not good. But at least they hadn't turned the search toward the mining camp. Yet.

"Dain, give me a hand," Scanner said.

Maro complied, helping the smaller man lift a capacitator onto the bench. Scanner busied himself with the heavy plastic device, and Maro stood back, watching. By tomorrow, according to Scanner, they could have one or maybe even both carts working. With luck, they could make the spaceport in another couple of days, if the projected speed of fifty klicks per hour came off. They had food—canned and bland, but nourishing—left behind by the miners. And they had enough fuel to run the carts for a week, if it came to that. If their luck held and the search didn't focus in this direction, they might make it yet.

But as Maro watched Sandoz doing a *kata* with the laser, cutting down imaginary opponents, he wondered if Stark and Karnaaj were the greatest danger at this point.

"Dead?" Stark repeated.

The voice of his search leader said, "Yessir. We found him buried in a sand dune. Wasn't for the transponder on the cycle, we probably wouldn't have seen him; he hit the sand pretty hard. Only the tail of the vehicle stuck out, and that not far."

"So it was an accident."

Karnaaj leaned forward in his chair, still as stiff as he ever had been, listening to Stark's conversation. The office seemed very quiet. The tropical night was falling outside, and the dregs of a rainstorm lingered.

"Uh, yessir, had to be. We got a call that he was having mechanical problems and he would try to make it back to base. Something must have glitched and he drilled in."

Stark felt his stomach flutter. It sounded reasonable enough; the aircycles were usually dependable, but they had not been designed to operate in full desert. The heat, the sand, anything could have caused a breakdown. There was the call, too.

But it felt odd.

"How did he die? Can you tell?"

"Well, there're no marks on him, except where the sand scraped away part of his face and shoulder. Looks like his neck and back and one arm were broken. He's got soft spots all over. I'm no medic, but it sure looked like the impact did it."

A beat. "All his gear still there?"

"Yessir. Pulse pistol, rations, radio, everything."

"All right. Continue the search."

After the discom, Stark turned to look at Karnaaj. The SDI man's face was, as always, unreadable. He asked, "Something bothering you, Warden?"

"You heard the report. One of my men was killed in a cycle accident."

Karnaaj shrugged. "Men die. It's part of being a soldier."

"Something doesn't feel right about it."

"Intuition?" The word seemed an insult.

"Maybe. That's the wrong way for the escapees to be heading. We know they have a compass, and there's no civilization for thousands of kilometers in that direction. But I only had one man checking that way before he crashed. Now, there's nobody."

"So send another man. It isn't likely they can hide on the desert."

"No. It isn't likely." Then again, he thought, it wasn't likely that anybody would ever escape the Cage at all, much less stay at large as long as this bunch had.

An excited voice broke into his thoughts. "Commander Stark!" It was the search leader again.

Stark looked at the com. "Yes?"

"We've found one of them!"

Both Stark and Karnaaj leaned toward the com. "Where?"

The man rattled off a series of coordinates. Stark punched up a computer map as he said, "Who? Who is it?"

"Was," the voice said. "He's dead. The animals and plants got to him pretty good, there's not much left, but the computer dentition matches the teeth to prisoner #769869."

Stark knew the numbers from memory. Berque. The map lit the holoproj field, and the coordinates flashed a blue dot over the location.

Southeast of the flitter.

Toward the desert.

Stark felt certainty building within him. "What about the others?"

"No sign of them. We have a vector, based on a line from the flitter. They're heading toward—"

"I know where they're heading," Stark snapped. "The desert. Concentrate your search in that direction. Half your men." He glanced toward Karnaaj, who nodded. "And half of Karnaaj's troops, too."

"Copy, Warden. Discom."

Stark clenched his fist. At last! They had a direction in which to look! But—why were they going that way? It made no sense.

"Computer," Stark said, "I want references to any human or mue settlements to the southeast of the on-screen coordinates."

It took less than a second. "No human or mutant settlements extant."

Just as he thought. Were they crazy?

Karnaaj said, "What about the mines?"

"What mines?"

"There used to be mining along the tilt of the edge plate, somewhere in that direction. We had a small detachment of men there six or eight years ago."

Stark stared at the terminal in disbelief. "Why didn't the computer say that?"

"Perhaps your question was not specific enough."

"Computer, list any human settlements or mining camps *ever* within two hundred kilometers southeast of the on-screen coordinates."

"None," the computer said imperturbably.

"*Dammit!*"

"A malfunction," Karnaaj said.

"Yeah, a malfunction! That droud-head Scanner is the malfunction! He's deleted information from the files!"

"Calm yourself," Karnaaj said. Stark came very close to telling him to go fuck a shrat, but managed to bottle it in time. "Why would they want to go to an abandoned mining camp?" the SDI officer continued. "They have to know we would check in that direction eventually."

"I don't know, but I'm going to find out!"

Even with power, they did not light the camp at night. Scanner had gotten a couple of battered hand lanterns powered up, and it was one of those Dain was using to search what had once been a military barracks. Raze had gone back to what had become their communal room to rest, and Juete followed Dain.

"What exactly are we looking for?" she asked.

Dain flashed the lantern's beam over the empty, stripped beds. The miners had left the mattresses, which had gone musty with mold, and the plastic frames, but little else in the long and narrow room. "I'm not sure," he said. "But I'll know it when I see it."

Juete looked. He had the light beam flared so that it threw a wide circle rather than a thin spot. "It doesn't look as though they left anything behind."

Dain walked the length of the room, shining the light into the dark corners. Something chittered and scrabbled away as they approached. She moved closer to Dain.

At the end of the barracks, Dain bent and poked the light underneath the bed there, looking under the springs and frame.

"What are you doing now?"

"I had a friend who was Confed Military for a while," he said. "He used to talk about things that they stashed for personal comfort. Sometimes it was a drug, sometimes other stuff."

"Wouldn't they have taken anything like that with them when they pulled out?"

"Probably. But it doesn't hurt to look."

Dain searched under another three beds before Juete spoke again. "It's Sandoz, isn't it?"

She saw him look at her in the dim reflection of the lantern where it bounced up from the floor. "Mostly, yes."

"If it's me—"

"It's not you, love. Sandoz is used to getting what he wants. He was willing to go along with me because I had a plan and he didn't know what it was. Now that we're out, he's getting antsy to do things his way. You're only a part of it."

A large part, she thought. She had not told Dain what Sandoz had attempted earlier, and had persuaded Raze to keep her mouth shut as well. Perhaps a confrontation between the two men was inevitable, but she did not want it to come any sooner than could be avoided.

Dain continued to look under the beds. Once he sneezed.

"Damned dust. Anyway, whatever Sandoz wants, he usually gets. He doesn't like taking orders, and sooner or later, he'll stop. He's too dangerous to fight. Not without an edge—ah-hah."

"What?" Juete leaned down and peered under the dusty plastic frame. There was what looked like a small circle drawn on the plastic of the frame, nestled in one corner. As she watched, Dain pried it loose. The thing he held was disc-shaped, about the diameter of a quarter-stad coin, but four or five times as thick.

"Hold the light," Dain said.

Juete took the lantern, and Dain held the thing in one hand and twisted it with the other. A cap came off in his fingers. Under it, a pencil-thick rod in the center of the disc protruded a few millimeters up from the surface. He turned the disc over, and there were what looked like fuzzy, hair-fine wires bunched up on the back.

"What is it?"

"A slap-cap. This matted stuff is adhesive. It'll stick to just about anything." He pressed the wireside of the thing against the palm of his hand. "See?" He waved his hand, and the disc stayed in place. "Pry it away slowly and it comes, but it resists sudden shear forces."

She still didn't understand.

"The rod, here, is the trigger. If you slap something fairly hard with this, it sets off a cone-shaped charge, equal to about a fifty kilogram punch, but concentrated into a small area. Hit a man solidly on the head or over the heart, kidney, or spleen—any place really vital—and it'll deliver a hydrostatic shock wave that will kill him."

Juete stared at the device, feeling her stomach knot.

"Slap an arm or leg, and it will shatter the bone and pretty much jellify the overlying muscle."

"What does it do to your hand if you use it?"

"If you're careless in your placement, it can break a finger or badly bruise a bone, but that's about it. The charge is newton-bleak—vents a lot of the reaction, I don't know how, exactly."

"The soldier wasn't supposed to have it," she said.

"Right. That's why he matched the bed's plastic for the cover. You'd have to be looking for it to spot it. I was, and I almost didn't."

"Your edge against Sandoz?" Juete felt cold and afraid. Dain was talking about possibly killing a man, and if it came to that, *he* might be in danger of dying as well. She didn't want to even consider that.

"Yes. My edge. I won't use it unless I have to, but it makes up for a lot. If he gets close enough in a fight—"

Juete stared at the device stuck to her lover's palm. She hated it; more, she hated what it was in men that made such things necessary. And at the same time, she was glad Dain had found it.

"Let's go back to the room," she said. It was suddenly very cold in the deserted barracks.

* twenty-four *

The radio's blare woke Maro. It took perhaps five seconds for him to make sense of what he heard. After that, all sleepiness vanished.

Raze sat up as Maro leaped out of bed. "What—?"

"Stark's men are on the way here! We've got thirty minutes."

Raze rolled out from under the covers and began dressing.

Juete said, "What's going on?"

Maro grabbed his orthoskins and slipped into them as he told her. In less than a minute he was outside the room, yelling for the others. It took another minute for them to gather around him.

"We've only got one of the carts fully operational!" Scanner said, still pulling on his coverall.

"How long to get the other one ready?"

"An hour or two—"

"We've got maybe fifteen minutes! We have to be gone when they get here!"

Sandoz glanced at Chameleon. The face-dancer nodded once and moved back toward the room he and Sandoz shared.

The rest of them ran to the two small carriers. Scanner

snapped on one of the portable lanterns, but Maro threw the power switch that lit the building. "Fuck it," he said. "We've got to move. If they get here before we leave, we won't have a chance. Can we all get into one of these things?"

"It'll slow the cart down, but yeah, it'll carry us."

"No it won't," Sandoz said.

Maro spun just in time to see Chameleon hand Sandoz the laser welder. Sandoz shrugged into the unit's power pack and switched it on. The needle of coherent light lanced out, a hard brightness under the artificial lighting.

"I'm taking the cart," Sandoz said. "Chameleon goes with me."

Maro glanced at the mue. Chameleon shrugged. "Sorry. He's better at staying alive, and that's what I want to do."

"And the albino goes with us," Sandoz added. He grinned at Raze, moving the laser beam back and forth in a lazy arc. It hissed in the quiet air.

Scanner pulled a small box out of his coverall.

Sandoz spun and aimed the tip of the weapon at Scanner's throat. He was three meters away, but two quick steps and he could skewer the smaller man easily.

"Whatever you've got there," the assassin said, "drop it."

Scanner grinned tightly and thumbed a control on the button. There was a *pop!* and spark from the laser welder's power pack. The red needle winked out.

Sandoz wasted no time trying to restart the laser. He shrugged out of the pack and dropped the ruined device. "You're just full of surprises, aren't you, wirehead?" He settled into a wide, low stance.

Maro reached into his pocket for the flare pistol. It wasn't there. He realized that it was still laying on the floor next to the bed, where he'd left it in case of an emergency.

"Never mind. I don't need the laser," Sandoz said

softly. He smiled. It was the expression of a man who was about to enjoy himself to the fullest.

Maro knew the assassin could take all of them. Raze was strong and the smuggler was a fairly good fighter, but Sandoz was a master. Juete and Scanner would only get in the way.

The slap-cap, covered against accidental discharge, still adhered to his right palm. He twisted the cap off slowly and extended his hand to the side, palm facing Sandoz. He let the man see the cap, could tell by Sandoz's expression that he knew what it was.

"Where did you get that?"

"It doesn't matter. I have it and you know what it can do. You might kill me, but I'll take you with me. Or a big enough piece of you to keep you from leaving here under your own power."

The moment stretched. If Sandoz attacked, they were all likely to die. Maro knew it, and he knew that Sandoz knew it. They didn't have time for this.

Sandoz said, "Into the cart, Chameleon."

"Huh?"

"Do it. You drive. *Move*."

Chameleon moved.

Sandoz backed toward the cart behind him, holding his hands in a defensive pose.

Maro's gut twisted. He couldn't attack—it would be much more dangerous than defense, and if he committed himself, Sandoz could probably kill him without taking a hit from the slap-cap.

Sandoz continued moving backward. Maro edged forward in a shuffle step, the cap held ready.

Chameleon started the cart. The engine whined into life and rumbled unevenly for a moment, then smoothed out.

Sandoz's legs touched the back of the cart.

"Go," he said to the mue. "Punch it!"

Chameleon obeyed. The slunglas tires screeched on the

plastcrete of the shop and the cart moved. Sandoz twisted and dived into the back.

Maro lunged after him, his palm raised to slap. Sandoz came up holding something in his left hand. He threw it at Maro. It was a food container; the heavy plastic carton slammed into Maro's upraised arm, just above the elbow, and the force of it spun him away. His feet tangled and he tripped. He tried to turn the fall into a dive, half-managed it, and hit hard on his shoulder. He squeezed his hand shut on the slap-cap, a stupid move. Fortunately, it didn't go off.

As he rolled over, Maro saw Raze sprinting after the speeding cart. Sandoz laughed and hurled another can. Raze swerved to avoid being hit in the face. It slowed her long enough so that the cart reached the exit. There was no way to catch it now, not unless Chameleon blundered into a wall or one of the rusted machines—which he didn't.

They listened to the engine fade into the night.

Maro came to his feet. "Can you get this one going?" he said to Scanner, pointing to the other cart.

"The ground drive already works," the circuit-rider said. "I can maybe get the GE machinery partially done so we can get some lift. We'll have to have it on bad ground."

"Whatever you can do in ten minutes," Maro said, looking at his watch. "After that, it won't matter."

"How long?" Karnaaj asked.

Stark looked at the clock in the guard tower. The two men stood on the wall, staring out into the night. "Five more minutes. If they're still there, we've got them."

"Five more minutes," Scanner said. "That's all I need."

Juete watched Scanner work by the light of the lantern. The building was dark again. The man moved at a frantic pace, twisting wires together, pushing circuit boards haphazardly into place, pounding with his hands on the delicate-looking gadgets.

"Is there any way we can keep them from seeing us?" Dain asked.

"I don't have time to rig anything to rascal their heat gear," Scanner said.

"I do," Raze said.

Dain turned to look at her. She held up something, and a small flame flared.

Juete said, "What good will that do?"

Raze grabbed one of the cans of generator fuel. "Just watch." She grinned, then turned and ran toward the exit.

"Dain? What is she doing?"

"She's going to set the camp on fire," he replied. "They won't spot human warmth in the middle of an inferno."

"Good idea," Scanner said, not looking away from his work.

"What?"

"Uh, that's affirmative, Warden. We've got a fire about three klicks ahead, right at where the mining camp is supposed to be. Big one. The whole sky is lit up."

Stark looked at Karnaaj. "What the hell is going on?" he said, more to himself than to the other man.

But Karnaaj answered. "I think our quarry is trying to pull something. Confound our sensors, most likely."

Stark said, "Then they *are* there! I want them alive, do you hear? Any of them turn up dead, whoever's responsible will pay with his ass!"

"Copy, Warden."

Maro silently urged Scanner to more speed. *Come on, come on—!*

Outside, the light from the fires Raze had set turned the night into flickering orange bright enough to see the entire camp. The smell of burning plastic assailed his nostrils, a sharp and bitter tang, and the sound of the flames was a dull, windy sound, shot through with crackles.

"That's the best I'm going to be able to do," Scanner said, leaning back. "If I had another twenty minutes—"

The hum of aircycles overrode the sounds of the fire.

"No time," Maro said. "We've got to move, *now!*"

"Where is Raze?" Juete said.

"We'll find her. Get into the cart."

The aircycles' sound grew louder.

Scanner pushed the ignition button. The cart's engine rumbled, but failed to start.

"Come *on,* Scanner—!"

The engine whined, rumbled, caught—then died. Scanner punched the starter again. The engine rumbled into life, stronger this time. Scanner engaged the drive. The cart rolled toward the exit.

"Ah, Warden, the whole camp is on fire. We've spotted one of them. The bodybuilder."

"Alive," Stark said. "Take her alive!"

Scanner drove the cart into the bright firelight, turned sharply to avoid an obstacle and nearly threw Juete out by doing so. She grabbed at the side. Dain caught her arm and pulled her back into her seat.

"Where is Raze?" Juete was in a panic.

"There!" Scanner said.

The woman was fifty meters to the left, running. Behind her, three men pursued. Juete heard the cough of a spetsdöd. Raze dodged, dived and rolled up, and kept going.

"Scanner!"

"I'm going, I'm going!"

He turned the cart toward the back-lit figures and throttled up. The cart jerked forward in a dusty haze as the tires tore up the dry ground.

Raze vanished behind an earthmover. The men chasing her skidded to a halt.

"Raze!" Juete yelled. "Over here!"

One of the men heard the yell. He turned, saw the cart bearing down on him, and raised the hand with the spetsdöd on it. Something clinked against the windshield of the cart. Scanner ducked and Dain tried to pull Juete down in her seat. She resisted. "*Raze!*"

As if in answer, the big woman suddenly loomed behind the man with the spetsdöd. She grabbed his head and twisted. Juete thought she heard the man's spine crack.

The other two men turned to see Raze. She lowered her head and barreled into them. All three went down.

Raze came up from the tangle of bodies. Juete saw her stomp down on one of them, hard. He screamed.

"HOLD IT!" came an amplified voice.

Juete saw a hovercraft above them. A bright spotlight arced out and threw its glare over Raze.

Raze sprinted out of the light, too fast for it to follow. Juete saw her outlined momentarily against a burning building.

A dozen men scrambled from the settling craft, which kept moving, dropping more troops in a human line that stretched past the fleeing Raze. She turned, running directly away from where the cart was.

Scanner turned the small vehicle to follow Raze, but there were troops and guards between them.

"Run them down!" Juete yelled.

Some of the men turned and began to fire at the cart. They weren't using spetsdöds, but pulse weapons. Bright beams seared the already fiery night, hard sounds and high energy dazzling to the ears and eyes.

Raze was trapped, her back to a melting plastic building.

"They want her alive!" Scanner said.

Raze looked up and saw the cart. She waved it away. "Go!" she yelled. "*Go!*" Then she smiled, a vulpine expression, all teeth. One of the men facing her raised a spetsdöd and aimed it at her.

"Fuck you!" Raze yelled.

She turned and ran into the wall of the burning building. Her body left a dark spot for a single heartbeat before the oozing plastic filled it in.

"Shear off!" Dain yelled.

The cart turned, skidding and throwing up a cloud of fine dust. Another pulse beam sizzled overhead, too high by a meter.

"They want us alive, too," Dain said. "Get us the hell out of here, Scanner!"

To their right, one of the burning buildings collapsed with a loud crash and a shower of burning plastic drops that rained down like shooting stars. Somebody behind them screamed. In the acrid smoke and conflagration, the pursuers must have lost track of them. Scanner drove the cart into the cool darkness past the perimeter of the flaming camp. He did not slow until they reached the forest.

Juete looked back at the camp as Scanner picked his way around the trees. Her tears flowed. "Good-bye, Raze," she said.

She glanced at Dain. In the faint gleam of the cart's instrument lighting, she could see that he was crying, too.

* twenty-five *

Stark stood at the door of his storage shed, staring at the palm lock. Dawn was coming, but the new day did not matter. Everything had gone to hell. Six more of his men were dead; three apparently killed by the dead bodybuilder, three more by the collapse of some building during the fire at the camp. It was small consolation, but eight of Karnaaj's men were also dead. The hovercraft in which they had been riding had been blown out of the air by the explosion of a fuel tank in a mining machine. Whatever chance he had of saving his career was gone. When the Confed finished with him, he'd be lucky to escape prison himself. The Confed did not like failure in its officers.

He reached up and palmed the lock. The sliding door, unused for years in the miasmatic tropical weather, squeaked and stuck halfway along its track. He grabbed the plastic panel and shoved it the rest of the way, then brushed his hand over the light plate. The overhead fluoros cast their hard glare down, filling the room.

Stark stared at the Juggernaut.

At first glance, it resembled a standard exoskeleton loader. The unit stood four meters tall, vaguely anthropomorphic in shape—two legs and two arms, with a torso big enough to contain a large man or mue comfortably. But the hands were not hydraulic clips, like a workmech's. The three pairs of "fingers" had been adapted for combat. One finger on the right hand contained the muzzle of a pulse weapon; one on the left had a flamethrower; the other pair of fingers could be used to pinch through plate durasteel or to pick up an egg equally well. Rocket launchers on both shoulders each held five heat-sensitive thermodrill Rodent missiles that could track more than fifty degrees from line-of-flight, once fired. The main body armor was five-centimeter-thick stacked molecular plasticast and could stop anything up to a 50 MM AP shell. GE repellors and bounce beamers gave the thing the mobility of a small jet to altitudes just below orbital. The control electronics and sensors were state of the art. It was a major piece of war machinery, and it had cost him the equivalent of a small fortune to come by it. The man who had "lost" it was dead, and nobody knew it was here but Stark. It was his final trump, and the time had come to play it. He would use the Juggernaut to find and kill all of the prisoners except Juete, and then he would use it to get them both to a ship and off-planet.

After that—well, he would have to play it as it came. He stripped his orthoskins away and punched in a code on the lock control of the exoframe. The machine hummed to life, and the hinged hatch swung smoothly open. A climatesuit lay neatly folded in the bodysleeve compartment inside. Stark donned the suit and triggered it into operation. He felt a cool pulse as the circulating fluids adjusted to the air and his body temperature. He pulled the hood over his head and tabbed it into place.

He took a deep breath. Once he climbed into the Juggernaut and slid his feet and hands into the extensors, his motions would be duplicated as exactly as the suit could manage. In a training test he had seen once, a skilled operator had squatted and picked up a tenth-stad coin from a smooth floor with the grippers, flipped it into the air and point-blasted it with the pulse gun as it fell. In personal combat, a man in a Juggernaut was almost invincible—save against another so armored. He was radar-ghosted, laser-reflective and had a cruising range of five thousand kilometers at speeds up to three hundred klicks an hour. Once he got inside and left, nobody was going to be bringing him back. Not even Karnaaj and all his men.

Stark took a deep breath and climbed up into the armored womb of the Juggernaut.

Dawn found them running smoothly to the north, skirting the desert, hidden in the trees. Juete had dozed off, and Maro leaned forward to talk to Scanner over the sound of the wind. Scanner had used the GE gear several times, and it seemed to be working, though he kept saying he didn't trust it to last.

"How long?" Maro asked.

"Couple more hours. We should find the end of the desert, if my maps are right. It's scrub land past that, not as much cover as the forest, but better than being a bug on the sand."

"Can we make to the port, Scanner?"

"Your guess is as good as mine. Maybe. No way to tell."

"If we get past the scrub, then what?"

"We go north until we hit the volcanic plain. Still a lot of activity there, a lot of heat and electrical flux, so even the satellites probably couldn't pick us up unless they just happen to footprint us directly. Which isn't very likely."

"I wonder how Sandoz and Chameleon are doing."

"I hope they're burning in some fanatic's hell," Scanner said bitterly.

"They were just trying to stay alive. We all were."

"Yeah, but we weren't trying to do it at their expense. Maybe the guards will follow them instead of us."

"Nice thought."

"Yeah."

They rolled on, using the GE gear over the rougher spots, bouncing on the tires otherwise.

Juete slept.

Stark walked into the fence surrounding Stores, not bothering with the gate. The electricity played over his outer shell harmlessly, and the wire tore like thread as he stepped through it. Automatic alarms sounded, loud in his amplified hearing. He turned the gain down on the suit's hearing. He grinned, in spite of his situation. This thing was powerful. Maybe he would not be as adept in it as was a trained operator, since he had only managed to practice with it surreptitiously a few times in the years since he'd acquired it, but still he felt unstoppable, and for the first time in days, his sense of helplessness fled. Let somebody try to stand in his way.

Nobody did. He saw startled guards, but none of them were so stupid as to fire at this monster.

He flipped the control for the GE and the bouncers. The chambers warmed and the repellors gave out a throaty growl, almost like a big cat's purr. He hit the thrust button and the Juggernaut leaped into the air.

His radio came to life with hails, but he ignored it. Some alert guard managed to trigger the manual wall lasers, and thin fingers of red stabbed at him, but missed by a dozen meters. He was tempted to fire a rocket at the guard's tower, or tickle the place with pulses, but decided against it. Some of the guards were good soldiers; no point in causing them any more grief than they were going to run into already.

He turned the Juggernaut away from the prison, climbed several thousand meters straight up and ordered the suit's computer to pilot him to the mining camp. He soared away, deadlier than the largest dragonbat that ever flew

Omega's skies, at a speed no living creature could hope to match.

The fuckers who broke out of his prison and ruined his life were going to be sorry they were ever born.

Juete was jolted awake as she leaned against Dain's muscular shoulder. She had been dreaming, but whatever the dream had been was gone.

"Where are we?" she asked.

"About a hundred kilometers north of the mining camp. They haven't spotted us yet, apparently. A cycle flew by half an hour ago, but it didn't slow."

She nodded. The reality of their situation was worse than any nightmare she could have had.

The radio came to life.

"This is Stark. Has anybody seen anything?"

Scanner slowed the cart slightly as he listened to the dialog.

"Copy, Warden. One of our teams found a broken-down cart about thirty kilometers south of the camp."

Scanner allowed the vehicle to slow to a halt. Dain said, "Well. It looks as if Sandoz's choice was a bit premature."

"Give me the coordinates. I am on my way."

That brought a sudden chill to Juete's neck.

"Ah, that might be inadvisable, Warden. It seems our men got careless when they were examining the cart. We have two dead on the ground and their weapons are gone. The cycles were coded, so they're still there, but the handguns weren't ID keyed. The escapees are armed."

"It doesn't matter," Stark's voice came back. "So am I."

"Go," Dain said to Scanner. "Maybe Sandoz and Chameleon can keep them busy long enough for us to get away."

Scanner throttled the cart up.

* * *

The guards at the small clearing in the woods where the cart had been found looked appropriately surprised and startled to see the Juggernaut settle to earth. The foot pads on the exoframe sank a couple of centimeters into the soft earth, but each had enough surface area to keep the thousand or so kilograms of the machine distributed enough not to cause problems. Some of Karnaaj's men were there, and they backed away. *Good,* Stark thought. He had no use for those troopers.

Stark's amplified voice boomed out at the men. "What have you got?"

The search team leader wiped his mouth with the back of one hand, looking up at Stark's face behind the plasteel plate. "Just like we said, Warden. Two dead, two pulse pistols gone. The tracks lead off that way. They can't be more than ten minutes ahead of us, we figure."

"Fine. Stay here. I'll get them."

He could have flown, but he wanted to use the machine to impress the troops. He turned in the direction of the escapees' travel and started to walk.

The brush hindered the hydraulic muscles of the Juggernaut no more than weeds would a man. Small trees fell under his mechanical feet; larger ones he shoved aside. He was able to move as fast as a running man, despite his great size, taking strides two meters at a step.

It took him less than ten minutes to catch up to them. He only saw two; Sandoz the assassin and the mue called Chameleon. They heard him coming; the metamorph cut to the left and ran, snapping wild shots from the pulse pistol at the Juggernaut.

Almost idly, Stark raised his left arm and triggered a blast from his flamethrower. A thin line of fire jetted forth and covered Chameleon with oily flame. There was a scream. The man ran in a small circle and then collapsed into a bonfire that moved feebly.

Sandoz snapped his weapon up and began firing. He

was good. Five for five hit Stark, starting at the belly of the Juggernaut and walking up to the faceplate. The last shot clouded the clear metal slightly to the left, but did no real damage. Stark aimed his pulse finger at Sandoz, but then decided not to use it. He moved ponderously toward the man, who kept firing until his weapon ran dry.

Sandoz was fast. He dodged as Stark reached for him. It took five minutes for the warden to run the prisoner down, and it was over that quickly only due to a lucky fluke: Sandoz tripped over a root and sprawled, and Stark caught him before he could scramble to his feet. The Juggernaut's mighty arms lifted the struggling man up so that their faces were level. Stark grinned at him.

"There's only one escape from the Omega Cage, Sandoz," he said. And squeezed.

Too fast and too hard—he didn't have the delicacy of touch of a trained operator. Bones cracked and Sandoz's chest collapsed. Blood gouted from the man's mouth and ears and he died instantly.

Stark dropped the body. *Damn.* He had wanted him to suffer more.

Scanner would. And Maro. Especially Maro.

He sprang into the air, repellors working, and climbed to three hundred meters. He put his sensors into full scan. His miniature holoproj heads-up display showed the troopers where he had left them, along with Chameleon's burning corpse and that of the crushed Sandoz. Several other animal lifeforms registered, but nothing that gave off the signature of a human. So. The others weren't here. They had split up.

It didn't matter. He would find them. There weren't too many directions in which they could run.

"Two of the prisoners died while resisting capture," he said. "Come in and pick up the bodies."

A hundred and seventy-eight kilometers away, Stark's

casual message reached the ears of the three remaining escapees. They looked at each other grimly, but no one spoke. The same thought was going through each of their minds: How could Stark take Chameleon and Sandoz—Sandoz!—alone?

With what was he armed?

* twenty-six *

Stark's radio buzzed with queries, mostly from Karnaaj; he ignored the calls and continued his flight pattern. He worked a spiral away from where he had killed Sandoz and Chameleon, his sensors turned to full gain. The Juggernaut's equipment was sensitive enough to tell a man from a large animal, were the operator of the exoframe properly skilled, but Stark was not an expert. Several times he dropped from the skies, only to find himself covering schweinhunds or sand cats. The last time, in frustration, he flamed the animals into cinders.

He flew over the desert, radar and doppler tracking the sand, looking for his prey. He would find them, no doubt, and when he did, they would die. Except for Juete, of course. She would hurt, but that would be later, when he had her safely off-planet. It would be a long time before she forgot this incident, and he looked forward to making her beg for his forgiveness.

Below, a sand cat started at the sound of the Juggernaut and loped off across the trackless waste, its big feet throwing up small showers of dry sand as it ran. He didn't bother to fry this one. That had been a loss of control before, and he did not want to let that happen again. He wanted to be calm when he found the last escapees. Filled with righteous anger, but calm. So that he could savor it.

"The lava plain is just ahead."

"How long will we be on it?" Juete asked.

Scanner said, "Most of the way. Fingers of it run almost to the edge of the mining port. It won't be as fast to stay on the plain, but it'll be a lot safer."

Maro stared at the plumes of smoke ahead, and caught the scent of burning sulphur, that characteristic rotten-egg smell.

"A couple of the volcanoes are still active," Scanner continued. "Nothing explosive, but some pretty good lava flows, according to the Cage's computer. And there are fumaroles bubbling all over the plain, especially close to the new flows." Scanner chuckled.

"Something funny?" Maro asked.

The circuit-rider glanced at him, then back at the plain. "Well, I guess it depends on your sense of humor. There was a little historical note in the computer on the early exploration of this planet. Seems the world was largely settled by gentlemen of fortune—mostly Confed ex-military—and there used to be a race held each year on the plain. Lot of hell-bent heroes would crank up some of the old hydrogen-powered land cruisers and tear across the hardened lava, to see who could get to the other side first. The last year it was held, sixteen of the seventeen cars disappeared. Sank in pits or got covered by a new eruption, it was figured. The only guy to finish came in first—and last."

"I don't think that's particularly funny," Juete said.

"Like I said, it depends on your sense of humor."

The surface of the plain seemed to be mostly black and bubbly looking rock, and it was quickly apparent that running it on wheels would pound them into jelly. Scanner switched to the GE mode and the ride smoothed.

"People used to race across this," Maro said. "Amazing."

"I think they had shock absorbers."

The pillowlike formations made for slow going—the repellors did not allow the cart much altitude—and the path had to be picked out carefully to avoid the larger hummocks. Maro's amazement that somebody would do this for fun was tempered by respect for the *langlaufers*' skill at being able to do it at top speed.

After an hour on the plain, they came to their first major obstacle. Along a gullylike path that had made for the easiest travel so far on the plain, they suddenly found themselves rounding a hill and facing a fifty-meter-wide pit of bubbling liquid rock. A blast of hot wind smote them, even though they were at least a hundred meters away.

Scanner touched a control and dropped back into wheel mode. He braked the cart to a halt.

"I knew this road was too good to be true," he said.

"Is that lava?" Juete asked.

"I would say so, yes. And we're going to have to turn back and find a way around it. I don't want to be cooked trying to cross it, thank you."

"You want me to drive for a while?" Maro asked.

"Not yet. When I get so tired I can't stay awake, then you can drive. Otherwise, I might as well do it myself."

They turned the car and began to retrace their path.

Stark flew his pattern, trying to stay calm, but growing irritated despite himself. Damn, where *were* they? If they had gone the same way as Sandoz and Chameleon, he would have found them hours ago. Therefore, the group had split up. Which way would they have gone?

Logically, he figured, they would have headed toward the closest starport, that being northeast of the Granite Girdle where the old mine was. But such a path would put them on the desert, and Stark didn't think they were that stupid—not after how canny they had been so far.

Sure, they could wander around on the planet for a while, but they had to know that he could find them easily if he kicked in search modes on the spysat system. No, they had to get offworld fast, just as he would have to do were he to survive.

How? What was the best way?

The exoframe computer was bright, for what it was. Tactics and strategy were its strong points. He asked it.

"Computer, plot the three most likely routes for a land vehicle to travel from coordinates 56-69-074 east to 57-23-112 west."

The computer's mechanical voice said, "Define parameters of *likely*."

"Routes that would be the safest for a small guerrilla force seeking to escape detection from air, land and spysat search."

"Capabilities of land vehicle?"

"Three-person surface quadcycle with supplementary low-altitude repellors."

The air in front of Stark's faceplate lit with the heads-up display. Holographic maps shimmered in the air. The three images each had a different route of travel marked by a glowing blue line. The maps were numbered, with one being the most likely path and three being the least.

The line on the first map led across the gigantic lava fields to the north.

Of course. All the piezoelectrical static associated with volcanic activity and rock movement would play hell with sensor gear. It might be dangerous on the surface, but the only way they'd be spotted would be by direct visual, which gave them a big advantage.

As much as he hated them, Stark had to give them credit. So far, the escapees had moved very cleverly.

Not cleverly enough, however. They hadn't known about his Juggernaut. He had figured out which way they went, he was sure of it. They'd make the smart move. Only this time, he wouldn't be a step behind.

He checked his position. He was on the southern arm of his spiral, unfortunately, and it would take more than an hour to reach the plain. By then, it would be dark. But that didn't matter. He would put the Juggernaut down and rest. In the morning, he would have plenty of daylight in which to find them. It was only a matter of when.

He gave the computer the coordinates, turned, and roared across the twilight skies.

Juete's buttocks were sore from the hard seat in the cart, and she rubbed them as they stepped from the vehicle. Dain had been driving for the last two hours, and the dark had finally forced them to stop. They did not want to use the lights; besides, they were exhausted.

Scanner pulled the heat tabs on three cans, and the scent of the warming food wafted to her. It might be bland by the Cage's standards, but nothing had ever smelled quite so good to Juete.

"How far have we come?" Dain said.

Scanner took a bite of what looked to be a reddish bean paste, swallowed and said, "About two hundred and fifty kilometers."

Dain offered a canteen to Juete. She took it and drank. "Not too good," he said.

Scanner shrugged. "Best we can do, considering the terrain. Thirty klicks an hour means we can make it to the port by dark tomorrow. If . . ."

"If what?" Juete said.

"If the repellors hold up."

"You think they won't?" Dain asked.

Scanner swallowed another mouthful of bean paste. He pointed at the canteen, and Juete passed it to him. He drank. "I don't know. They ran hot for the last couple of hours. We can drop to the ground, but given the topography, we'd be lucky to do ten klicks an hour."

Juete leaned back against the relatively smooth chunk of

black stone. She was exhausted; so much had happened in the last few days. She hoped they would make it, hoped they would be able to escape from Omega, but if they didn't, if they were tracked down, she knew she was not going to return to the Cage and Stark's perverted sense of love. She would die first. And somehow, that did not seem as terrible as it once had been. The albino Exotics had a highly-supported sense of self-preservation—another legacy from their creators. One did not wish to lose such a valuable possession through suicide, after all. But there came a time when death was preferable to life, perhaps. Or, at least, a time when the quality of life might not be worth the struggle. Suicide, no. But fighting to preserve her freedom and others', even to death, yes.

That had been Raze's decision, after all. She could do no less.

Next to her, Dain slipped his arm over her shoulders, as if suddenly sensing her mood. She snuggled closer to him, looked at his face, then glanced over at Scanner. Dain would not mind, she knew, if she invited Scanner to huddle with them. It was the three of them against the world, after all, and what comfort they could take together, they should.

But before she could speak, Scanner said, "I'm going to sit in the cart for a while." He stood, stretched, and walked the ten meters to the cart.

Juete glanced at Dain.

He said softly, "He's going to link to the cart's computer. It isn't much, but he gets something from it."

She nodded. She could understand that.

After a while, without speaking further, she fell asleep against Dain.

Maro gently moved away from Juete, easing her head down onto the jacket he'd found at the camp. She slept hard, not stirring.

He climbed the boulderlike rock behind them. It was easy enough, the moons' light was bright, the sky clear. It was maybe twenty meters to the top, a soft incline, and from the pinnacle he could see kilometers in any direction.

Here and there, reddish-orange glows lit the sky. And twice in five minutes, bright discharges like lightning flared whitely. Such an eerie landscape, like something out of a prehistory holovid. He almost expected to see dinosaurs stalking across the hardened lava, or a herd of curlnoses lumbering past. Below him, Juete slept, while Scanner communed with his electronic spirits. Maro felt very much alone on this alien plain. So far away from anywhere he ever thought he would be. He thought about the others who had trusted him to lead them to freedom. Four dead—five, counting Fish, who had never even managed to climb the walls. Sandoz, Chameleon, Berque and Raze. Raze most of all he was sorry about.

The sadness welled in him, filling his chest and throat, and it almost overcame him. No. Not tonight. Later, maybe, if they lived, later he would have time to mourn properly. For now, he needed to concentrate on staying alive. Otherwise there would be no one to pay respect to the others.

He climbed back down the rock and stretched out next to Juete. It was cold and hard, but sleep finally came.

* twenty-seven *

Stark awoke, and for a moment did not know where he was. He felt panic close in until he remembered. The Juggernaut lay on its back, and the seat padding made it as comfortable as any other field cot he'd ever slept in, albeit somewhat limiting insofar as motion.

He touched a control and the repellors hummed as they lifted the suit to a standing position. He clicked the exit controls, waited until the hydraulics opened the clamshell doors and climbed out.

He looked about the landscape, bleak and desolate as a moon. He stretched, relieved himself, and jogged around a bit. The morning sun was only beginning to show over the horizon. He reentered the Juggernaut, sat in the control seat, and fastened the unit tight again. The water from the mouth tube was cold and clean, and the nutrient paste was warm, if somewhat tasteless. It was sustaining, however, and that was all he needed. He reconnected the penile catheter and powered up the flight mode. Even the computer could not say exactly how the fugitives would cover the ground, since detailed maps were not available, but that was unimportant. He would head northwest, zigzagging. It would take a little longer to cover a fifteen-klick-wide swath, but in the end, he would catch them.

The Juggernaut lifted amid a spray of volcanic rock dust, a giant raptor on the prowl.

Juete had almost gotten used to the rhythm of the cart's swaying flight as it dodged rocks too high to hop. Scanner was driving again, and for a time, the plain was flat enough for nearly top speed. An hour after they started the ground ridged again, becoming more convoluted. She wondered how it had come to be formed that way. Were there some underlying rocks which had become encysted? Or did the cooling lava pile up on itself? It was not important that she know, but it did make her curious.

Next to her, Dain stared across the plain, not speaking. He seemed far away this morning, lost in his own thoughts.

In the middle of a particularly rough stretch of ground, Scanner stopped. "Got to rest the GE," he said. "It's overheating."

Juete looked around. The surface reminded her of a stormy ocean she'd once sailed over on another world; it was as if someone had frozen the wind-driven waves into stone. There were peaks and troughs and a thousand different shapes surrounding them.

They had passed several more fumaroles, pits that exuded hot and stinking gases or bubbled with molten rock and mud. And yet, even among the solid rock and killing heat, she had seen plants. They were mostly small, stunted blobs of gray-green, some kind of lichen or moss anchored to the rocks at odd angles, usually in shaded spots. Even in the midst of such desolation, there was life. Some kind of a lesson there, wasn't there? The sun beat down, but it was cooler than the desert when they were away from the fumaroles. Juete wore a flat-brimmed hat Dain had found at the camp, and slathered herself every few minutes with sunblock. Even so, she felt her skin burning where it was exposed to the light.

After half an hour, Scanner restarted the cart and they moved on.

Maro trusted Scanner's driving more than he did his own. Scanner plugged into the cart's simple computer and controlled the vehicle directly, for the most part. But the concentration required for the interlink was hard on the man, and Maro offered to spell him every hour or so. Scanner looked drawn, tired, and he had lost probably five kilograms since the escape. They were all wearing thin, Maro knew. If they couldn't get to some kind of safety within another day or two, the stress would burn them out. The price paid for constant fight-or-flight was too much to continue for long.

"Dain?"

Maro turned to glance at Juete. Scanner was asleep in the back next to the beautiful albino. "Yeah?"

"Listen, no matter what happens, I want you to know I love you. I appreciate what you've done for us. For me."

"Thank you," he said.

He somehow felt better, even though nothing had changed. Win or lose, he had done what he'd had to do.

Back and forth Stark tacked, flying a Z-pattern that extended seven and a half klicks on either side of a straight line toward the mining port. He looked at the land below from an altitude of a hundred meters. The suit's sensors worked sometimes, and sometimes they did not. Once he had been nearly over a large fissure that had suddenly ground shut, and only his polarized faceplate had saved his eyes from the actinic flash of a giant spark as it leaped from the ground and floated up past him like ball lighting. His sensors had gone off the scale.

But, even though he could not track the escapees, there

were very few places for them to hide. He would see them among all the ripples and valleys of the slag, sooner or later.

He worried for a time that they might have fallen into one of the steaming lava pits, but he somehow did not think that Fate would cheat him so.

Methodically he flew, back and forth, searching.

As the afternoon wore toward dusk, Scanner stopped the cart more and more frequently. Finally, an hour before dark, with the shadows stretching over a landscape grown more and more mountainous, they halted.

"That's it," Scanner said wearily. "The GE gear is dead. If I had parts and tools, I might be able to fix it. But we've burned a rotor and there's no way we can continue on hover."

"It's okay," Dain said. "You pulled off a miracle getting us this far. We'll just have to do it the old-fashioned way, on the ground."

Scanner looked around. Juete was shocked at how thin and gaunt the man's face appeared. "We'll move like snails. There's hardly a centimeter of flat ground as far as I can see."

"We'll manage. We can always walk, if we have to."

"It's about forty kilometers, I figure," Scanner said.

"We crossed that much desert, didn't we?" Juete put in.

"Yeah. I guess."

"Should we stop, do you think?" Dain asked.

Scanner shrugged. "Might as well go until dark."

"Okay then. We roll."

Stark's anger could not be held back. Where *were* they? He had not missed them, he was sure of it! And yet, the spaceport lay only another fifty or sixty klicks ahead. Surely they couldn't have gotten that far yet? They had to be on the plains still. But darkness was coming and there was still no sign of them.

A yellow fog seemed to cover the ground ahead.

"Better avoid that," Scanner said to Maro, who was now driving. "Could be sulphur dioxide. Probably has a lot of carbon dioxide in it, too."

Maro turned and began to circle the gas cloud. They had been lucky; they had managed to travel another fifteen kilometers on a winding but fairly flat stretch. But darkness was making the driving treacherous, and now Maro decided to halt for the night. He pulled the cart to a stop in the shelter of a tall spire of rock. *Almost there,* he thought. *We're almost there.*

Stark cursed the darkness. And then, he saw something on his scopes.

He had gotten a number of ghosts and bad readings since he'd entered the lava fields, but this looked like the readings of three large, warm-blooded animals. He had seen nothing like this on the plains until now.

It had to be them. It *had* to be!

The darkness would not impede him if he chose to take them. The Juggernaut was equipped with spookeyes, light intensification equipment that would allow him to see in almost total darkness. He could pluck them from the dark as easily as if it were midday. But no. Now that he had them, he wanted to make it last. Now that he knew where they were, they couldn't outrun him.

He climbed, wanting to be hidden in the night, and flew past the position of the prisoners.

"What was that?" Juete asked.

"What?" Dain's voice was sleepy.

"That noise, didn't you hear it? It sounded like a jet."

Dain shook his head. "Probably a fumarole venting gas."

Juete strained her ears, but the noise, whatever it was, was not repeated. "Yes, I guess that must have been what it was."

But she felt an icy touch within as she lay curled next to the man she loved. It followed her into sleep.

In the morning they started off again, bouncing along the pitted rock, jolting around in the cart like insect specimens in a shaken bottle.

Scanner was driving. He saw it first.

"Jesus," he said softly. "What is *that*?"

Ahead, directly in their path, stood a monster.

✶ twenty-eight ✶

As Maro watched, the monster raised one arm and pointed an extended finger at them. In that second, Maro realized what it was: some kind of armored exoskeleton. And at the same moment, he knew who rode within—Stark!

This was what had killed Sandoz and Chameleon.

"Out of the cart, fast!" he yelled.

Scanner locked the brakes. The little cart skidded to a stop on the hard black rock. Scanner jumped to the left, while Maro shoved Juete out to the right and followed her.

The cart rocked as the front was blasted by a pulse beam. Hot plastic bits sleeted through the air. One of them landed on Maro's shoulder, burned through the orthoskin coverall and raised a blister.

He didn't slow, but urged Juete behind a block of lava two meters tall. Behind them, he heard an amplified laugh.

"It won't do you any good!" the warden's voice thundered.

"It's Stark," Juete said.

"Shhh, he might be able to hear us."

The responding laugh echoed across the lava. "He's right, my love. I can hear your faintest whisper! I can hear your heartbeats, if I want. Although Maro and Scanner won't be having any in a few minutes."

Juete stared at Maro, afraid. She grabbed his arm tightly with both hands. Maro didn't think she was aware of her move.

"You can come out, Juete. I won't hurt you."

Even with the electronic distortion, Maro could hear the voice soften. He caught Juete's hands. "I don't think he'll hurt you. You could give yourself up—"

"No!"

As if in answer, the rock shuddered. A few pebbles rattled down the side and hit them as the pulse beam baked the opposite side of the stone.

"Look out!" Scanner yelled. "He's coming!"

The warning wasn't necessary. Maro felt the footfalls of the massive exoskeleton reverberate through the ground. He grabbed Juete's hand and tugged her away from the boulder, keeping it between them and the approaching Stark. They ran, dodging around small rocks. A pair of honeycombed black pillows three or four meters tall loomed ahead to the left. They made it to the nearest and ran behind it.

A line of fire arced between the two rocks and drew a burning bar upon the ground. In a moment, another line bracketed the opposite side of the rock, and then a third fell on the far side of the block next to them.

"Careful, Maro—you might get burned!" Stark yelled.

Juete and Maro looked at each other. *He's got us boxed in,* Maro thought, *and he knows it.*

Inside the Juggernaut, Stark grinned widely. Oh, this was going to be wonderful!

Something pinged off the back of his helmet. What—?

He checked the rear display. There stood Scanner. Throwing rocks!

Stark laughed. Give the little runt credit for balls. He knew he was dead, and this certainly was a stylish way to go—better than cringing behind a boulder. He turned the

Juggernaut to face Scanner, raised one arm and prepared to pulse the circuit-rider.

Then he paused. No. He didn't want to kill him just yet.

Scanner bent and picked up a fist-sized chunk of rock. He drew back and threw. The rock sailed past, half a meter to Stark's left. Stark extended one arm and fired the pulse. A lucky shot—the rock exploded into powder.

He turned back toward Scanner. He shifted his aim to the man's right a meter. There was a knee-high boulder there. He opened up with the pulse finger, and the rock blasted apart. The concussion and a certain amount of lava shrapnel hit Scanner and knocked him flying. The man fell, sprawled on his back.

Stark locked his sensors onto Scanner and turned the sound up. Still breathing—there was even a hint of a heartbeat. He grinned and lowered the volume. *I'll come back for you later, little man. You can watch as I pull the arms and legs off Maro, one at a time. Then I'll do the same for you.*

Stark turned back toward the two big rocks. The ground heat would screw up the tracking systems on his missiles, but he could use line-of-sight. He turned and flipped his aiming scope on at the same time. He centered the rock to the right in the crosshairs of the scope. Fire one!

The little missile streaked away and slammed into the rock. The explosion caused his sonic sensors to cut out with the overload, so the sound was damped, but he saw the little rocket blow a man-sized chunk out of the boulder with a satisfying cloud of dust and rock. That ought to stir them up some.

He strode forward, taking giant steps, and rounded the corner of the rock, hands set to grab.

They were gone!

Dammit! While he had been playing with Scanner, they had slipped away!

Stark turned the Juggernaut slowly in a circle, looking.

Nothing. He triggered his sensors, but there was a pond of smoking lava not fifty meters away, and the heat overloaded his electronics.

No problem—he could always take to the air and spot them, but it might be more fun to stalk them on the ground. There were only so many rocks, and they couldn't outrun him.

Yes. That was what he would do.

A row of low ridges, almost like wind ripples four feet high, bordered the lava pit on the north and east sides. Dain had led Juete there, and the two of them crouched among the ridges now, with smoke and heat haze making it hard to breathe. "It'll be hard for him to walk here," Dain whispered.

Juete nodded. Whatever happened would happen to them both. There was no sign of Scanner, and she was afraid that Stark had already killed him.

Dain pointed.

Stark was fifty meters away, on the opposite side of the lava pool, moving at a right angle. Dain motioned for her to get down.

"Why doesn't he just lift?" Dain said. "He could find us easily."

"Too easily," Juete said. "He wants us, but he wants to make it last. I know how he thinks." She didn't say what else she knew was true: once he had them he would kill Dain and then take her, next to Dain's body. It would excite him. She felt sick.

Dain said, "That faceplate looks pretty thin. Either it's plasteel or densecris, I can't tell which."

"What difference does it make?"

"Maybe none. But part of the faceplate is cloudy. Looks as if it was damaged somehow."

"How could you have noticed that?"

To her surprise, he grinned tightly. "One notices all kinds of odd things when one is running for one's life."

"You think it might help us," she said. "But how?"

"Densecris is almost invulnerable. But plasteel is metal, and it vibrates differently . . ."

Stark, now that he had them pinned down, had all the patience in the world. They could hide for a while, but sooner or later he would spot them.

Maro and Juete circled when Stark turned in their direction, keeping low. The lava was abrasive, and Maro bled from half a dozen small scrapes on his hands and arms where he had stumbled and hit the sharp-edged rock.

They ran back in the direction of the cart once Stark was on the opposite side of the lava pool, where the heat would obscure his view and—Maro hoped—his sensory instrumentation. There they found Scanner, sitting in front of the cart. He had a plate removed from over the steering mechanism.

Scanner shook his head when he saw them. "I always knew you were clever," he said to Maro. "You and Chameleon, you could have gone into business together."

Juete said, "What are you doing?"

"Fixing the cart. All his shot did was take out the steering motor on the right. If I can cross-circuit the left motor, we can drive."

"Drive where?"

"Who the fuck cares? We don't have a prayer on foot!"

Maro said, "We don't have a prayer in that, either. He'll spot us easily and we can't outrun him."

"You got a better idea?"

Maro bit his lip. "Yeah. One. But it depends on Juete."

Juete did not hesitate once Dain had explained his plan. "Yes," she said.

"It's risky."

"It doesn't matter."

* * *

Stark's joy in the hunt was beginning to fade. He had been at this for half an hour, and he had nearly had it with playing cat-and-mouse. He could climb up on one of the tilted slabs of lava and spot them, most likely.

He was near the south end of the lava pond, staying well back from the unsafe-appearing lip that rimmed the pool, when he saw Juete. She was standing no more than twenty meters away, her back to an oblong rectangle of lava that was canted from the ground at a sharp angle.

He stopped and caught his breath. Gods, even dirty and with her clothes torn, she was beautiful. She said, "Stark? Don't kill me, please."

Kill her? How could she think that? His resolve to make her suffer dissolved as he watched her, so frail against the black rock.

"I made a mistake," she said, her voice tinny and contrite over the exoframe's speakers. "I was afraid. I—I love you, Stark, and I was afraid of the power that would give you when you found out."

His heart raced. She loved him! It was what he had wanted to hear her say since the first time he had touched her!

He started forward. He would put her somewhere safe, on top of a hill, and finish the other two quickly. Then he would take her and get the hell away from this damned planet!

So engrossed in her was he that he almost missed the movement to his left. Scanner! The little son-of-a-shrat was still alive!

And, while he was watching Scanner, preparing to coat him in flaming death, he felt something leap onto his back.

The Juggernaut's gyros compensated—he could carry several tons, easily, and there was no chance he would lose his balance. There came a pounding, as if someone was hammering on his back. He twisted, but could not see. He flicked on a pickup, and the angle was enough so that he just could see Maro on his back, slamming at one of the shoulder missiles with a chunk of rock. He was trying to set the rocket off!

Stark felt a moment of panic, and reached up and over his shoulder to grab Maro. The man ducked, slid partway down, and Stark missed. He could have simply fallen onto his back then and crushed Maro, but he didn't want to lose his chance to kill him slowly with the Juggernaut's mighty waldoes.

Stark spun and slung Maro off with the speed of his move. Maro fell, scrambled up, and tried to run, but fell again, favoring one leg, which had evidently been hurt in the fall. And then Stark was on him. He bent and grabbed Maro, catching him under the arms, lifting him off his feet. At last!

He turned toward Juete, lifting Maro so that the man was held at arm's length. He said, "So. You love me. That's why you tried to attract my attention so Maro could sneak up on me. That hurts, Juete. And so I'll have to hurt you. Watch what happens to your lover."

"Stark! Don't! *Please!*"

Stark looked at the struggling Maro. "You're a dead man."

Maro said something, but Stark didn't catch it. "What's that, dead man?" He squeezed slightly.

Maro went limp.

Stark shook him. Had he applied too much pressure again, as with Sandoz. Or had he simply fainted? He looked at the data readouts, but the heat from the nearby lava pool still rendered them ineffectual. He turned up the directional sound gain. The prisoner's heartbeat was slow, very slow. Stark moved Maro closer, looking at him through the plasteel plate, searching for signs of consciousness. As he watched, the man's eyes snapped open, staring directly into his—and he smiled. Smiled! *I'll give you something to smile at!* Stark thought.

He started to squeeze . . .

Maro slapped his open palm against the faceplate. Stark caught an instant's glimpse of a flat disc hitting the plasteel, and then a hammer of sound and pain slammed into his face. He screamed, and instinctively dropped Maro and brought his hands to his wounded face. A mistake, since the Juggernaut duplicated his actions, and the powerful waldoes clanged against the plate, making things worse. Gods, it hurt, it *hurt*—! He felt something running from his left ear, and there was a black crater on the plasteel in front of his left eye. His head throbbed. He backed away, stunned. What had happened?

Maro stood and threw a rock at Stark. The rock bounced off the faceplate.

Damn you, damn you, *damn you!* Stark lunged, hit the ground five meters away, just short of Maro, and fell. Maro turned and ran.

Stark got up, his head ringing, his face hurting, and lumbered after the man. He raised both of the behemoth's hands.

Maro dodged as Stark let go with both the flamethrower and the pulse guns. Lava splashed, on the ground and beyond in the pool, as the pulse fingers spewed power. Stark tried to track Maro, twisting, but nearly fell. The exoframe's gyros were not compensating well—perhaps whatever Maro had done had damaged the electronics.

He slowed, regained his balance, and swung to cover the man. There he was, standing next to the lava pool.

Juete ran in front of Maro.

Move, Juete! Stark thought. But he could not speak, his head hurt too much. Her hair flew up from the heat of the pool. He couldn't shoot, he would have to reach over her and catch Maro in his hands again. He took a step forward—

And the lip on the edge of the pit crumbled. He canted sharply to his left, falling. He hit the surface of the lava, broke through a thin crust of drier material, and felt heat wash over him like a wave of fire.

He had to get out! The exoframe would melt!

He triggered the repellors. He felt them start, whirr, then die. No! The lava had damaged them! Or maybe it had been Maro's rock, earlier . . . he struggled, trying to right himself by pulling at the crust of the lava, but it only gave way under his hands. He could feel his skin baking—the pain was unbelievable, intolerable. He was sinking.

"*Juete!*" he screamed.

And sank beneath the surface.

"*Run!*" Dain yelled.

Scanner was already moving. Juete turned and began to sprint. Dain caught her hand and, despite his limp, urged her forward, faster.

"Get behind that rock!"

They stumbled behind the oblong block of lava, sprawling next to Scanner. Then there was an explosion that rocked the ground. Lava sprayed past, flinging melted rock in a thick sheet.

"The suit," Scanner said.

Juete understood. The power reactor of the exoframe Stark had worn had exploded.

A rain of metal and rock snowed down around them. Part of a human hand landed a meter away from Juete. She screamed.

Dain turned her. "Don't look," he said. "Don't look."

✳ twenty-nine ✳

The rest of it was, comparatively, almost easy.

Scanner nursed the wounded cart back to life. It took several hours to reach what civilization the spaceport offered.

Civilization was run by computers.

Scanner found an access port and had passes issued to them. If anybody was curious about how they looked, nobody spoke of it: the passes indicated that they were a priority-cleared party and that to delay them was a mistake.

What they stole was a Confed Military shuttle, big enough for a dozen men, but small enough to pilot easily. Amid the hails from the tower demanding clearances, the ship lifted. "To hell with the noise restrictions," Scanner said.

They were almost into sling pattern when the com buzzed again. Somebody who had the private codes wanted to talk.

Scanner glanced at Maro. Maro shrugged. "Go ahead."

The lean face of a Confed commander lit the screen.

"Karnaaj," Juete said softly. But they had not opened their transmitter to send on visual mode: he couldn't see them.

"This is Karnaaj. Who is lifting in my ship?"

Scanner laughed.

"Give him a picture," Maro said.

The circuit-rider's fingers danced over the control board. "Done."

They watched Karnaaj's face turn gray when he saw the visual. "You!"

"That's right. Us," Juete said.

"But—but—Stark . . ."

"His fighting machine ran out of luck," Maro said. "So did he. And it looks like you might have the same problem."

"You'll be blasted from the sky!"

Scanner said, "Not by anything the Confed's running in this sector." He tapped the droud on the side of his head. "You've got a massive computer failure, Commander. Even the killsats are taking a rest."

Karnaaj slumped back in his chair.

"Give our regards to the Confed," Maro said. "I think you'll be talking to them real soon."

"Wait," Karnaaj began. "Wait, please—"

Scanner killed the connection.

In the silence save for the muted roar of the lifters, the three looked at each other. "We made it," Juete said.

"Looks like it," Maro said.

Scanner grinned. "Ain't that a spin?"

They all began to laugh as the stolen ship cleared the atmosphere of the planet Omega, to fly into galactic history.

Nobody had ever escaped from the Omega Cage.

Until now.